WHEN THE WHISTLE BLOWS

When The Whistle Blows

by

Ailie Scullion

Dales Large Print Books
Long Preston, North Yorkshire,
BD23 4ND, England.

British Library Cataloguing in Publication Data.

Scullion, Ailie
When the whistle blows.

A catalogue record of this book is
available from the British Library

ISBN   1-84262-069-X pbk

First published in Great Britain by D. C. Thomson 1995

Copyright © Ailie Scullion 1995

Cover illustration © Melvyn Warren-Smith by arrangement
with P.W.A. International Ltd.

The moral right of the author has been asserted

Published in Large Print 2001 by arrangement with
Ailie Scullion

Dales Large Print is an imprint of Library Magna Books Ltd.

Printed and bound in Great Britain by
T.J. (International) Ltd., Cornwall, PL28 8RW

Beth Stewart, Staff Nurse

The auburn-haired staff nurse needed to stand on tiptoe to check her appearance in a mirror, set high on the staffroom wall. The majority of Beth Stewart's colleagues came of Highland stock and were tall. Her own lack of inches, at times like this, caused her minor irritation.

The infirmary at Fort William was expecting another busy day. The first train from Glasgow would bring a fresh batch of men, each one hoping for work on the West Highland Line's new extension. It was a feat of railway engineering which had been under discussion for a long time, and at last, in the closing years of the century, approval had been given to make a start.

The men would have been travelling for days, some from isolated villages in the Highlands, others from across the Irish Sea – navvies, tunnellers and the like. Successful candidates would be arriving at the town's hospital all day for their routine medical check-ups.

At a first glance, it was difficult to believe Beth Stewart was twenty-two years of age, or indeed that she was a fully-qualified staff nurse. Her naturally curling hair made a glowing halo about a heart-shaped face, and when she smiled, dimples destroyed any illusion of seriousness.

Alec Buller, the new doctor in charge of casualty, had finally stopped teasing Beth about her diminutive appearance. He had now seen her in action on the wards, and realised she was a capable assistant and an invaluable asset to the hospital staff.

Lately, Staff Nurse Stewart had been singled out by Alec Buller. The less charitable amongst the nursing staff could be heard to say that she had set her cap at the doctor since the day he arrived in the Fort, straight out of Medical School in Edinburgh. He certainly showed little interest in any of the other nurses.

Needless to say, these remarks were never made within earshot of Beth, whose temper could match her red hair, especially when accusations were unjust. Straightening her starched cap now, Beth headed for Matron's office.

'Ah, Nurse Stewart. Here is our list for today.' The frown on Matron's brow softened as she looked at her young assistant. Staff Nurse Stewart had a way of inspiring confidence. She was a boundless bundle of energy and seemed to take everything in her stride.

'Oh, we'll get through it, Matron. Those

WHEN THE WHISTLE BLOWS

At last work was starting on the desperately needed extension to the West Highland railway. None could have guessed, least of all Beth Stewart, how much it would change her life.

poor men out there look so tired. I'm sure they'll be as glad to get it over as we will.'

The older woman watched as the nurse ran a practised eye down the list of names.

'Tunnellers mostly, I see,' the girl remarked. 'Father said they were expecting a new lot today.' Beth's father had helped build the West Highland's original line to Fort William, and afterwards had been kept on by the company in a maintenance capacity, while he waited for the new extension to start.

Already the waiting-room was filled with men. Those who could not find a seat leaned against the walls. From her desk, Beth studied them closely. She could tell at a glance which occupation they were likely to follow. Navvies, for instance, were renowned for their outfit of cloth cap, a muffler knotted around the neck, and corduroy trousers supported by a stout belt and fastened under the knees by leather 'yorks.'

A bell announced the start of examinations. Beth called out the name of the first man on her list, then ushered him into the surgery where the duty doctor awaited. During these examinations Dr Alec Buller worked quickly and methodically, his concentration never wavering as he skimmed through the pages Beth handed him.

Once, when the patient had gone into the

9

side room, Alec straightened up, pressing a hand to his aching back. 'Good grief, Beth, where do they all come from?' he said, lowering his voice, and a grin spreading across his tired face. 'By the way, is it all right for Saturday?'

Beth's dimples appeared immediately as she smiled. 'You know me, Doctor. I never pass up the chance of a free meal.'

The young doctor had received an invitation for two to attend a dinner being organised by the railway's board of governors in the town's biggest hotel.

'Even if it includes a boring lecture about safety regulations?' he teased.

Beth's chin lifted. 'My father says, so far as he's concerned, there cannot be enough safety measures on that line. The work's fraught with danger.'

Beth had been little more than a schoolgirl when her family moved to the Highlands from the city, after her father was appointed tunnel foreman. Despite safety precautions, there had been several accidents caused by cave-ins.

A sigh escaped the white-coated man opposite. 'So speaketh the railwayman's daughter. All right, Nurse Stewart, bring the gentleman in.'

From his window-seat in the third coach, a young, dark-haired man stared out. For a moment Shaun Nolan could scarcely take in the spectacular view of the cone of Ben Dorain. It was difficult to believe that he'd been privileged to help build the first stages of this famous scenic railway.

Directly ahead of the engine, a broad valley separated the train from the mountain. It was at this point the Company had planned its famous Horseshoe Curve, where passengers could look across the valley and see the line just traversed, a pall of smoke marking their passage.

Shaun Nolan had left Scotland once his work on the tunnels finished. He still remembered arriving here from an isolated village farm in the south of Ireland, a callow youth of sixteen, innocent of the ways of the world. It had been his good fortune, and no doubt aided by a fond mother's prayers back home, that he had fallen under the protection of Rob Stewart. That man had been like a father to him, he mused.

The train passed over another viaduct, and with an expert's eyes Shaun noted how the thick, stone walls had stood up to passing years, recognised arches he'd worked on by the side of his experienced journeyman, and a swell of pride filled his heart. Men on the line used to say when you worked with rock, you finished up with some of it in your veins.

The young man grimaced and noted his

reflection in the window, the square set of a chin and a firm mouth which had once been known for its ready smile. Nowadays, Shaun Nolan hardly smiled, and the haunted expression rarely left his pale eyes.

He was not an old man, just twenty-seven last month, yet sometimes he felt he was carrying the world's troubles on his shoulders. People expected a man to be strong inside as well as out, but there were times when he felt like crying. He wondered now what his bosses would say to him turning up two days late for his interview, even if he had the strongest excuse. There had been things to attend to, legal forms to be signed and goodbyes taken.

When Rob Stewart wrote to tell him about the new extension and the job that awaited, Shaun had already been on his way home from Canada, after hearing that Rosa was ill. The letter from his Scottish friend remained unopened, left for him on the mantelpiece of his mother's parlour. Truth to tell she had enough on her plate with wee Julie to look after.

Rosa! A physical pain shot through his body. Shaun blamed himself for that, too. He had let Rosa down badly, that wonderful girl whose loving heart wasn't matched by a constitution that would stand up to the rigours of his windswept homeland. He told himself he should have seen this before

12

setting off for Canada to earn money. Rosa was used to sunnier climes.

On the day he should have been attending his interview in Scotland, Shaun Nolan stood instead on a barren Irish hillside at his young wife's funeral service. He'd arrived just too late to be with her at the end.

Little Julie, mercifully, was much too young to grieve. She just gurgled and cooed, safe in the arms of his own mother. It was taken for granted the child's grandparents would stand by Shaun in this, his time of need.

'You get off and sort yourself out, lad.' His father had spoken brusquely, for he was not the type for soft words. 'Your mammy and me will look after the child.'

The tattoo of iron wheels altered as the train slowed down. They were entering a station whose platform was bedecked by pot-plants.

'Bridge of Orchy!' the porter cried.

Shaun watched a straggle of passengers board the train. He realised that the next stop would be his own, although before reaching this, he would travel across some of the most barren and desolate countryside imaginable – the moor of Rannoch.

Oh, my old friend, Rob, he pondered wearily, and stared out of the window as the train moved off. I wonder what you'll make of your former apprentice now?

When her morning shift ended, Beth hurried to pick up her cape, and was about to leave the hospital when she heard footsteps behind her in the corridor.

'Where are you off to in such a hurry?'

She swung round on her heel. 'I told you, Alec, I'm going down to the wharf to see my brother. His boat's been laid up for weeks there, and I didn't even know.'

The young doctor tapped his forehead. 'Sorry, forgot. Still, I can walk you part of the way. I've need of some air.'

'If you like.' The invitation seemed half-hearted, and Alec Buller looked down at his small companion. 'You know how it is with Will and my folk, Alec. I have to tread carefully.'

The man striding alongside shrugged. He was an only child himself, so found it difficult to understand family squabbles.

'You don't mean to tell me that feud is still going on?'

'Afraid so,' the girl replied wearily. 'I don't know who's the more stubborn, my father or Will.'

'And just because your brother prefers catching herring to working on the railway. Seems crazy to me, Beth.'

Beth shrugged. She was loyal to the core, but she agreed with Alec's opinion, although she wouldn't dream of saying so. It seemed daft to fall out over something so trivial, yet her father was adamant. Will had gone off to Mallaig and signed on the herring-boats, after Rob Stewart had used all his contacts to get his son on to the railway's pay-roll.

'Never let the sun go down on your anger.' How often had she heard this said in the Stewarts' home? Yet, three years had passed, Will had his own boat, and was married to his boss's daughter, but had not even thought of asking his family to the wedding. It had been the final insult. The rift widened.

Beth and Alec stopped for a moment at the top of the hill, and looked down over the busy railway terminus with its piers and dry docks.

'I hardly ever get the chance to speak to you nowadays,' Alec grumbled.

'I'm under your feet all day, up there.' Her dimples appeared as she pointed towards the drab, grey building where they both worked.

The young doctor frowned. 'Ay, but it's all business up yonder. "Yes, Doctor, no Doctor, will you look at this chart, Doctor?"'

'Would you have it otherwise?' she retorted primly. 'Anyway, we're not in the hospital now!' Her words sounded provocative, and he gazed down at her suspiciously then saw her dark eyes dancing as she pointed to their left.

'One of these days I'm going to call your bluff. I've things to say to you, Beth Stewart, but they're not meant for waggling ears.' He'd caught her hint – a row of interested spectators, in the shape of workmen who'd come to eat their packed lunches in the fresh air, were seated on a wall not far from where they stood.

'I told you, Alec, I have to see Will. It's urgent. Anyway, we'll have lots of time to talk after we go to your fancy dinner on Saturday.'

'I'll hold you to it!' Alec retorted.

He left her to walk the rest of the way on her own, watching as she skipped sure-footed down the cobbles towards the harbour.

Beth carried her own lunch-box under one arm. Her work at the hospital was demanding, and Janet Stewart was of the opinion her daughter did not eat enough. Normally, Beth was glad to settle down and eat her sandwiches in the little staffroom set off the wards, put her feet up and take a well-earned rest. Today, however, she'd arranged to meet Will.

Two fishing boats were tied up, side by side at the far end of the pier. Catherine II, at first glance, seemed a sound enough craft, but she'd been in repair now for the past three weeks. It was only by sheer chance Beth heard that a small fishing boat had been rammed in a fog. This would be her third visit to the quay in the past week. If it were the last thing she would do, Beth was going to make her brother see sense. As she drew near, the recent repair work became visible, with new wood replacing the hole in the hull just above the waterline.

On seeing Beth's approach, a tall man left the wheelhouse and came on deck to greet her. 'Beth!' Two strides took the fisherman to the rail. He swung himself over it then down on to the quay.

'How's my baby sister then?' Will Stewart set his head to one side and examined the petite, uniformed girl from head to foot.

'Not so much of the "baby", if you please. I turned twenty-two yesterday, in case you didn't remember.'

Her brother looked contrite. 'I didn't forget, Beth, honestly, but I've had more on my mind lately than birthdays.'

Beth felt her heart constrict as she gazed up at him. Eight years her senior, Will was already showing premature signs of silver at each temple.

'How is...?' she began.

'Mhairi? Ah, Beth, it's nice of you to inquire. If you must know, I'm really worried about her. She's eight months pregnant, and things haven't been going too well. She doesn't get nearly enough rest, what with all those brothers of hers, not to mention her father.'

There had been virtually no communication between the Stewarts and the McCallums, but since Will's boat was laid up, Beth had learnt a few things. 'I wish you could find a place of your own, Will. It's not fair on Mhairi having to live in her father's house.'

'I know that fine, Beth!' Will rubbed a hand across his bearded chin. 'They're a selfish bunch, the McCallum men. They've been used to being waited on hand and foot, and since their mother died, it's all landed on poor Mhairi.' He stopped short, but Beth knew intuitively what was on his mind.

Robert Stewart insisted that his son had made his own decision and now could abide by it. Will was dependent for his very existence upon his father-in-law, who owned a small fleet of trawlers sailing out of Mallaig. Mhairi's brothers skippered most of them, and Will had been entrusted with the old man's boat after he'd retired.

Reading between the lines, Beth felt the McCallum family were taking advantage of her brother. His earlier knowledge of engines must have come in useful when old Fergus gave him charge of his ailing trawler.

'You getting the short end of the stick, again, Will?'

Will nodded his head towards the boat

18

tied up alongside. 'I'm told the hull has been passed as seaworthy, Beth. At least that's one worry off my mind, but I'm not absolutely sure of her engines – they could do with a major overhaul. The thing is, I can't afford the lay-off.

'Once my crew arrive, we'll have to sail,' he went on. 'Now, if my father's favourite railway company would just hurry up and build that extension to Mallaig, I wouldn't have to travel so far to discharge my catch, and I could spend more time with my wife.'

The fishing skippers, especially those registered at Mallaig, had been crying out for the railway extension for years. Politicians kept delaying the project's start, and getting their catches to Fort William in time for transporting to the markets was an added burden for the fishermen. It was while doing this that Catherine II had been caught in a fog while manoeuvring her way to moorings. Only Will's skill had brought her safely to shore.

Will helped Beth aboard and led her to his cabin. She produced her lunch of chicken sandwiches and shared them with her brother.

Will smacked his lips in appreciation. 'You eat well, I see,' he commented.

'Mum keeps hens and geese behind the house now. I wish you'd go up and see her,

Will. She hasn't been too well, lately.'

Her brother looked up sharply. 'What's wrong?'

'I don't really know, Will. She won't go and see a doctor, but she gets tired easily.'

He looked at his sister suspiciously. He wouldn't put it past Beth to make him feel guilty about his long absence from the Stewart home... Yet, if his mother was really ill...

'Look, I'll think about it. Is Father working up the line right now?'

Beth hesitated. 'Well, no. He's here, in town, for the recruiting of tunnel men. They're being interviewed today.'

Will pursed his lips. 'I'll have to think about it.'

Beth was about to leave when her brother thrust out a restraining hand.

'Just a minute, lass. I've something for you in the locker.' He reached upwards and pulled out a parcel. 'Something Mhairi knitted for your birthday. See, we didn't forget.'

'Oh, Will, how kind of her – of you both. I'll write and thank her,' the girl promised.

'She'd appreciate it, Beth, really she would,' he said with a catch in his voice.

Glancing at the watch pinned to her tunic, Beth let out a gasp. 'I'm late again! I'll have to fly, Will, but promise me you won't sail again until you're sure about those engines.'

He looked at her fondly. 'You're such a worrier, little one. Off you go and tend to your patients.'

Her cape flying behind her, Beth hurried up the hill. As she ran, she realised with a pang that Will hadn't made any promises.

The town, Beth noticed, seemed full of jostling figures today. Another train had just arrived with its cargo of men hoping to work on the railway.

When Beth's father came with the engineers to work in the area, the Fort had been a small, backward town with an unhappy military history. Since the West Highland Railway had made its terminus here, it had developed into something of a tourist centre, partly because it nestled at the foot of Britain's tallest mountain, Ben Nevis, and boasted some of Scotland's best fishing.

Loch Linnhe, with its access to the sea, also drew visitors from more northerly isles, including the fleets of fishing boats tied up at the piers.

The afternoon list was almost complete when the man came hurrying into the waiting-room. Dr Buller looked up impatiently. 'Take a note of the man's details, Nurse Stewart.'

She sat down at her desk and drew the pad of forms towards her.

'Name, please…'

There was a long silence and she tapped her pen impatiently, then looked up. The man at the other side of the desk was staring down at her with the palest grey eyes she had ever seen. There was something about him that looked slightly familiar.

'It's Beth, isn't it? Rob Stewart's little Beth?'

She was aware that Alec Buller had swung round to discover who this forward young man could be. She gave the newcomer her full attention.

Her father was for ever bringing folk from his work up to their house, and her mother would provide a meal for them, but this one seemed different. For one thing, he sported a deep tan, one which had never been acquired in these parts. Workmen in the Highlands were more weatherbeaten than tanned.

'Shaun Nolan! I worked with your father for five years. I was his…'

'Boy wonder!' The words slipped out before Beth could stop them, and once again she became aware that Alec Buller was listening attentively. Her father had often spoken about the youth who had been his apprentice in the old days, the Irish youngster he'd taken under his wing and who was as smart as they came.

'And what are you doing back here, Mr

Nolan?' she asked now. 'I thought Father said you went abroad.'

'I did,' he told her simply, 'but now I'm back and I've been to see the contractors. They say I've to have a medical, but…'

'That's why we're here, Mr Nolan,' Alec Buller put in sarcastically.

Shaun Nolan had perched himself on the end of Beth's desk.

She looked up briskly. 'Then I'll just ask you to fill in this form and go into the side room and strip to the waist.'

The Irishman seemed bemused. The last time he had seen this girl she was at school, a tiny wee thing with unruly red hair and freckles. Certainly, Rob's last letter had said his daughter was now nursing at the infirmary. Otherwise he would never have recognised her.

'If you wouldn't mind, Mr Nolan,' Beth prompted. 'We're running late, and the doctor wishes to examine you at once.'

'Would you give my regards to your father?' Shaun asked over his shoulder. 'I'll be getting in touch with him soon, for there's something we must discuss.'

He seemed embarrassed, Beth thought, puzzled, then turned back to her work.

When Shaun Nolan left after his examination, Beth stared thoughtfully after him. She was remembering when he had visited their house years ago, a carefree youth, always laughing and singing in that rich, Irish voice of his. Today, he'd seemed a different man – as though he carried the worries of the world on his shoulders.

Then she shrugged. She had troubles enough of her own right now, what with Will's problems and niggling worries over her mother's health.

Alec Buller re-appeared at her desk. He handed the man's card to her for filing.

'Another fit specimen if ever I saw one, but why he wants to crawl about damp tunnels beats me, after working in the sun all these years.'

When the doctor returned to his surgery to clear up, Beth glanced curiously at the information detailed on the card – Shaun Nolan... Age twenty-seven... Position interviewed for... Beth's hand trembled as she checked the card again. How could he! She knew now why Shaun Nolan had looked embarrassed earlier. After all her father had done for the man!

Suddenly she could not wait to go home. There were things she had to tell her father.

There had been no sign of remorse on Shaun Nolan's face, yet he must have known what his arrival was going to mean to her father.

Her shift had come to an end, and she could see Alec Buller approaching her, a hopeful look on his long, lean face.

'Walk you home, Beth?' He did so occasionally, although it took him well off the route to the room he'd rented in town. Beth's generous-hearted mother invariably asked him to stay for dinner. Alec admitted that he loved to join the family around the kitchen table and enjoy a home-cooked meal.

'If you don't mind, Alec, not tonight,' Beth excused herself. 'I've something I must discuss with my father. It's sort of private.' She could see immediately she had hurt him. 'I'm sorry,' she attempted to apologise. 'I'll explain tomorrow, but I really must speak to my father first.'

'No need to explain anything,' Alec broke in stiffly. 'I'll – I'll see you in the morning.'

Janet Stewart carried a pot of boiled potatoes to the sink and drained the water from them. Tonight, she'd made Robert's favourite meal, mutton casserole with carrots, and there was bread and butter pudding to follow, but she could see by his face that he didn't have an appetite.

She'd watched him pace up and down after he'd returned from work, and although she felt sympathy for his plight, Janet was not quite so disappointed at his latest piece of news.

'Five years I've waited for this oppor-tunity, Janet. Five years, working for the

Company on a reduced wage, and they promised me three years ago that I'd be the first to be considered!' he reminded her.

'Ay, it does seem unfair, dear, but maybe your age–'

He rounded on Janet sharply. 'What's my age got to do with it? I'm only sixty-one and as fit as I ever was.'

'Well, perhaps Sh...'

'Go on,' her husband urged. 'Don't be afraid to mention his name, Janet – Shaun Nolan, the lad I trained when he scarcely knew what a tunnel was. I taught him everything he knows, and now look what he's done. He's stabbed me in the back and taken the job I was promised without even so much as a word of apology!'

They heard the sound of feet on the flags outside.

'That will be our Beth.' Janet looked at Robert urgently. 'Try not to let her see you're so disappointed.'

He continued to stare at her moodily...

'I read his card,' Beth told them later as they sat around the fire, the girl's face now as serious as her parents'. 'To think that I was pleasant to the man when he arrived, and all the time...'

'Perhaps he didn't know about your father, dear...'

'Oh, he knew all right,' Robert Stewart interrupted. 'I heard it all being discussed while I stood outside the office, waiting to be seen. They were saying how he's got specialised knowledge now, what with his jaunts abroad, and how he was experienced in this new idea of using concrete, instead of the natural stone. Of course, it helped when Nolan explained how he'd worked before with the extension's new contractor.'

Nothing, it seemed was going to placate her husband.

Janet Stewart gave a weary sigh and crossed to the sink to begin the washing-up. Beth joined her. 'I've been giving more thought to this business, Mum,' she began. 'Perhaps it's all for the best. Look how you worried about Dad in the old days when he was tunnelling. It won't be his responsibility any more.'

Janet spared her daughter a pitying smile. Beth was obviously trying to put a brave face on it, she thought.

'He has his pride, lass. Can you see him taking orders from a man who was once his apprentice?'

'It's a low trick Nolan played on him,' Beth agreed. 'And to think how we used to treat him…'

'Ay, Robert treated him like a son.'

Beth's hands flew to her mouth. 'Talking about sons, Mum, I saw our Will again today. He's really unhappy about the way things are between us, and he's worried about Mhairi, too. Don't you think it's about time we all made our peace?'

Janet rubbed a hand across her brow. 'Nothing works as easily as that in this family, Beth,' she said wearily. 'Your father and Will are too alike – stubborn as they come. Rob got Will that apprenticeship in the engine repair shop as a favour, but your brother's heart was never in it. The first chance Will got, he was off to sea, and your father has never forgiven him.'

Beth sighed. 'Oh, Mum, I know that. I've heard it all a hundred times! It's just wrong that our family isn't pulling together.'

Her mother nodded. 'Ay, if only we could turn back the clock, Beth. I wish we'd never left the city. There are times I still feel like a stranger here.'

These rebellious words troubled Beth. It was the first time she'd heard her mother admit to being unhappy with her lot. Janet Stewart had always seemed content living in the Highlands, and when her husband went off tunnelling, she'd filled her days with self-imposed chores.

But now, Beth remembered quiet moments when her mother would talk of her earlier life in Glasgow, where there had been grand shops to visit, real department stores with winding staircases and restaurants that sold tea from silver pots.

Beth herself could remember little about

city life. She'd been so young when they moved after her father started working for the railway company. There had certainly been a change in her mother over the past few months, she reflected. Normally a woman of tremendous energy, she now seemed a shadow of her old self. Climbing stairs would leave her short of breath, and Beth had been pleading with her for weeks to have a complete check-up.

'What do I want to see a doctor for?' Janet Stewart would argue. 'There's nothing wrong with me that a good holiday wouldn't fix.'

Her mother had accused Will and her husband of being stubborn and hard to reason with. If the truth were known, she was just as bad, refusing to consider that she could be in less than perfect health.

'Anyway, promise me you'll speak to Father about Will?' Beth said now.

Janet Stewart hesitated. 'It's hardly the right time, Beth, what with all this bother about his job, but I'll think about it,' she conceded.

The sound of the door-knocker being rattled caused the older woman to swing round. 'Now, who on earth can this be?'

Rob Stewart had a disturbing habit of inviting railway friends home without so much as a word of warning, and they would invariably turn up in the middle of a meal.

The Stewarts' cottage sat at the top of a hill. To its rear, a garden where Janet kept her livestock meandered into the hillside. To the front, however, there was an uninterrupted view of Loch Linnhe, and in summer months this could be idyllic. Tonight a strong wind was driving sheets of rain from the sea-loch below.

Why would any of her husband's cronies tackle the hill on such a night? Nevertheless, Janet glanced at her reflection in the mirror then, pulling off her apron, hurried into the hall, Beth close on her heels. But Rob Stewart had beaten them to it and was about to usher someone inside.

A Confident, Mature Man

The new arrival was a tallish woman in her mid-twenties. Bedraggled and dripping, she stood hesitating in the porch. Her long, dark hair had been tossed about in the strong wind and gave her a wild gipsy look.

Beth took in the situation immediately. The wide-fitting tweed coat which the woman was attempting to hold in place failed to disguise the fact that she was pregnant.

As she stepped into the light of the hall, Beth's first impression was of a beautiful woman with dark eyes and high, fine cheekbones, but she also noticed the unhealthy pallor of the woman's skin and deep shadows under her eyes.

Strangely, when the young woman spoke, there was no sign of weakness in her voice, rather a note of defiance. 'So, you're Will's folk. I wouldn't have come, you understand, things being as they are, but there was no-one else to turn to. I'm Mhairi, your son's wife.' As she spoke, the young woman seemed to sway on her feet.

Beth recognising the signs of sheer exhaustion, rushed towards her, arms outstretched, and was just able to break Mhairi's fall as she sank to the floor in a deep faint.

They laid her gently on the settee which Rob and Beth pulled over in front of the open fire.

Beth began to undo Mhairi's outer garments as her mother came rushing back with smelling-salts.

'Oh, Mum!' Beth exclaimed. 'Her hands are blue with cold.' She began to rub circulation back into them, as her mother tucked a blanket around the shivering woman.

'What on earth is she doing here in the Fort, Beth, and on a night like this?'

31

Robert Stewart's expression was one of deep embarrassment. He looked on helplessly as his wife and daughter attended to Mhairi.

As the smelling-salts passed below her nostrils, Mhairi began to cough and tried to sit up. 'What happened?'

'Hush!' Beth urged. 'Take your time now.'

The colour was beginning to return to Mhairi's cheeks. 'I was at my wits' end,' she began in a few minutes. 'You see, Will left Mallaig three weeks ago, and I haven't heard a word from him.'

She hesitated, biting her lip, and the three Stewarts could see that she was deciding whether to explain further.

'Will and my father had a row, you see. Poor Will, he'd already taken more than enough. He accused my father of penny-pinching and told him he would never allow one of his own sons to sail the Catherine II.'

Rob Stewart stiffened. 'Are you saying my son has been sailing a boat that's unseaworthy?'

Mhairi didn't seem to hear his question. Now that the floodgates were open, she seemed unable to stop. 'You should have heard them both,' she went on. 'Father was claiming Catherine II had always been the pride of his fleet, but Will gave as good as he got.

'"Ay, maybe so, Fergus, but that was ten

years ago. She's only fit for the scrapyard now", he said.'

Beth felt uneasy about the flush of colour which stained Mhairi's cheeks. She touched her sister-in-law's hand. 'Try to stay calm, Mhairi, and tell us why you've come all the way up here. Surely Will didn't send you on a night like this?'

'Will?' Mhairi spoke vaguely. 'No, Will didn't send me. My brother, Saul, did. He said he would have to go out with the others to check on a distress signal, and he suggested I should come here and wait.'

Rob Stewart drew closer. 'Did I hear you say that Will has been here in town for three weeks – and hasn't called to see us?' he demanded harshly.

His daughter-in-law gave him a strange look. 'Would you have welcomed him, Mr Stewart? I was under the impression you'd washed your hands of Will years ago.'

Beth decided to take the initiative before the situation grew more fraught.

'I saw our Will at lunch-time,' she said.

Her father rounded on her. 'You, too? What sort of conspiracy is this?'

Beth sighed. 'No conspiracy, Father. I was merely trying to patch things up. He said he might come by to see you.'

'Kind of him, I'm sure.'

'Oh, be quiet, both of you!' Janet Stewart bent over Mhairi. 'Can't you see this girl is

33

at the end of her tether?' She took Mhairi's hands and held them in her own. 'Be assured, lass, Will can come up here any time he likes and be made most welcome, despite what this foolish man of mine likes to pretend.'

Mhairi let out a strangled cry. 'If it's not already too late, you mean?' she asked in a voice that trembled.

Janet Stewart shook her head. 'I don't understand, lass. What are you trying to say?'

Mhairi took a long breath. 'I sailed from Mallaig on Saul's boat at first tide this morning,' she explained. 'It turned really stormy halfway, and I felt so sick I just wanted to die, but I thought it would be worth it, if I could just see Will again. I've been missing him so much.'

'There, there, lass. Don't cry.' Janet put her arm around Mhairi's shoulders.

'If you must know, I've been desperate for advice. I'm due to have my baby in four weeks' time, and since Will and I married, we've had to live in the family house with four men,' she went on. 'Mrs Stewart, I just wanted another woman to talk to. Will said Beth was a nurse and she might be able to help.'

'That goes without saying,' Janet assured her soothingly, 'but tell me, please, why is Will not with you now? I can't believe he would send you here on your own.'

Mhairi's eyes filled. 'No, Mrs Stewart, I'm not with Will, because the Catherine II is no longer in dock. She sailed with the tide, just hours before we arrived, and I'm worried sick. You see, the weather is closing in fast, and Saul says there are gales forecast.'

There was a stunned silence in the Stewart cottage, the family inside staring at one another. Rob's face was ashen. 'Janet, this is my fault. I drove our son away, and look what's happened. Perhaps it's a judgment.'

His wife could find no words of comfort for there was truth in what her husband said. She glanced anxiously at Mhairi, still lying on the settee and being comforted by Beth.

Janet decided that this was no time for recriminations. 'Hush, Rob, Mhairi's in a bad enough state as it is.'

Rob gave her a scathing look. 'Why shouldn't we be worried, Janet? Will is out there in a crippled boat, and there are gales forecast!'

Janet grabbed at his arm urgently. 'I know that, too, Rob, but we must try to keep calm for her sake.' She drew in her breath sharply as she remembered something. 'Didn't Mhairi say something about a distress signal?'

'Ay, Janet, I believe she did.' Rob went

hurrying back to the fireside, but Beth, who'd overheard their conversation, forestalled any further questioning.

'Dad, Mhairi's utterly exhausted. I think we should let her rest for a bit before we ask her anything else.'

Reluctantly, Rob agreed. He began to pace the floor. Each time he reached the window, he would pull back the curtain to stare out.

'Look, I can't stand this any longer!' he exclaimed at last. 'I'm going down to the harbour. Perhaps there will be some news.'

Mother and daughter watched in silence as he pulled on oilskins, then, with a wave of his arm, went out into the night.

The two women stared at one another.

'Mother, surely Will won't come to any harm?' Beth began.

Janet signalled worriedly towards the settee, but Mhairi appeared to have fallen into an exhausted sleep.

'Will told me himself he wasn't happy about the boat's engine,' Beth explained with a worried frown.

The older woman pressed her lips together. 'Well, if there's something wrong, our Will is the very person to put it right.'

For the short while he'd worked for the railway company, Will had developed a remarkable skill with steam engines. His foreman had been sorry to lose such a skilled employee when Will decided to change jobs.

Rob had felt keenly that Will was wasting his natural ability.

Beth's lips tightened. 'No wonder the Mc-Callums welcomed him with open arms!' she said tartly.

Janet shook her head. 'Hush, Beth. There's been enough of that sort of talk. Anyway, your father and Fergus McCallum are both stubborn men, neither willing to back down. I daresay Will has been trying to keep the peace for Mhairi's sake.'

They heard the sound of a sob and hurried back to the fireside. Mhairi Stewart was sitting up, the expression in her eyes showing her anxiety. 'I fell asleep,' she admitted in distress. 'How could I sleep at a time like this?'

Beth took hold of her sister-in-law's hands.

'You slept from sheer exhaustion, Mhairi,' she told the other girl gently. 'Now, are you able to tell us any more, dear? I believe you said something about a distress signal?'

Mhairi nodded. 'A fisherman reported a flare out in the Sound, but he was in trouble himself. His boat was carrying a full load and taking in water. He couldn't turn back.'

Beth's face lit up. 'But, don't you see, Mhairi! If that was Will, then the boat must have been afloat. Surely he'll have headed for one of the islands to take shelter?'

The three women stared at one another,

then Mhairi spoke the thought which was in all their minds.

'Ay, if the engine lasts out until he gets there...'

'I'll make us some tea.' That was Janet's answer to most emergencies.

Later they huddled close to the fire with mugs in their hands.

'My husband has gone down to the docks to see if there is any news, Mhairi,' Janet said. 'Did you say your brother, Saul, was going out to search for Will?'

The young woman looked up. 'Yes, Saul's the only one who has ever tried to get Will a fair deal. The others closed ranks.' Her words sounded bitter, and Beth and her mother remained silent.

'It's true, you know,' Mhairi went on. 'He's my own father, but anyone in Mallaig will agree that Fergus McCallum is a hard man. Will has been telling him for months about Catherine II. He said if he could be allowed to work on her for a few weeks, then he could put her right. But oh, no, Father said they could not spare the boat, that the catch would suffer, and they were getting little enough return for their labours these days!'

Beth's small face tightened.

She remembered the conversation with her brother earlier that day, when he'd admitted his father-in-law was insensitive, especially about his own daughter's needs. Mhairi was heavily pregnant, yet the man expected her to cook and clean for them all. What sort of man would do that to an only daughter?

Rain swirled around the sheltered harbour where a large fleet of fishing boats was tied up, crews busily battening down hatches and making their crafts secure. The harbour-master's office was crammed with men, all dressed in oilskins. Jock Sims, who'd been fishing out of the Fort all his working life, was speaking.

'I'm sorry, Mr Crossan, but it would have been useless for us to go out again while the weather's like this. Saul McCallum will tell you himself.'

A red-haired fisherman nodded glumly and turned to the harbour-master.

'It's true what Jock says, Mr Crossan. I tried for over an hour but heavy seas drove me back. I had my own crew to think about, you understand. We had to abandon the search.'

Rob Stewart allowed his grief to get the better of his reason. 'Is that it, then? Have I to go home and tell my wife and your own sister that there's no hope of finding my son alive?'

Saul McCallum's cheeks turned the colour of his hair. 'I hardly think that would be wise, sir, and unfair to Mhairi, if I may say so. Anyway, there is still hope,' he pointed out. 'Will is no fool. If I know him, he'll have headed for one of the islands and be sheltering in a bay.'

'Ay,' Rob Stewart conceded, 'if his engine gets him there!'

Saul McCallum stroked his chin thoughtfully. 'Catherine II was one of our first boats converted to steam. She was my father's pride and joy, and he was of the old school, insisting that she retain some sail-power. If all else failed, Will could have used the sails.'

At his words, Rob looked at the young seaman hopefully. 'Do you really think that's possible, McCallum?'

'It's what I would have done in similar circumstances. As soon as the weather settles, Mr Stewart, we'll be out looking for him again, you can rest assured. Meanwhile, I suggest we all try to get a few hours' sleep?'

Saul McCallum was not given to speeches, and his crew gazed at their skipper with new respect.

Rob, despite his doubts, realised there was sense in what the younger man said. 'All right,' he agreed gruffly. 'I take your point, but I think you should come up to my house and explain all this to your sister and my wife. We can give you a bed, and when you go out again in the morning, I'll come with you.'

The fisherman looked doubtful, but one look at Robert Stewart's face told him it would be useless to argue.

It was one of the longest nights Beth could ever remember. She'd had to share her bed with Mhairi, and both women tossed and turned for hours.

Beth listened as the wind whipped against the windows, and thought about Will. She prayed and prayed that he would survive this wild night, and when sleep still would not come, finally got out of bed and pulled a cardigan over her nightgown.

'You got it then?'

The voice from the bed startled Beth.

'The cardigan I sent with Will for your birthday,' Mhairi said.

Beth realised she had grabbed the first thing that came to hand, and now studied the garment closely. It was knitted in an intricate pattern and in several shades of wool. She'd noticed Will had worn a jumper knitted in a similar pattern.

'I used to knit for all our men,' Mhairi went on with a wistful smile.

Beth's heart went out to her sister-in-law. 'I think it's beautiful, Mhairi. I'm glad to have the chance to thank you for knitting it for me. Now, you said earlier that you wanted to speak to a woman about your pregnancy. Well, I'm here and ready to listen,' she urged.

Mhairi shook her head. 'Thanks, Beth, I'd like to do that, but first I must know if Will is safe.'

With this, Beth had to remain content. Later, when she went to peer out from the window, she noticed that the sky had begun to lighten and that the wind had dropped considerably. She heard the sound of a door closing downstairs, and saw two men leave the house. She recognised the bulky frame of her father dressed in oilskins and the tall, spare figure of Saul McCallum, his red hair standing up like a halo around his lean face.

Looking at her watch, Beth realised that it was now Saturday – her one, precious day off. Tonight, she realised wryly, she was supposed to be going to a dinner with Alec Buller.

Shaun Nolan found himself digs in the Fort William station-master's house. The contractor's agent had arranged it all after he was appointed tunnel foreman for the new extension.

It was a comfortable room at the top of the building, and boasted a cheerful, coal fire and a window that leaned out over the roof. He wasn't due to start his new job until Monday, and had been given the weekend to himself.

Although glad of the break, Shaun did not take much pleasure from it. He still had Rob

Stewart on his mind, and the sooner he met up with the man, the better.

Shaun was no coward and wanted to tackle the unpleasant task without delay, but the Company had asked him to speak tonight at some meeting at a local hotel. They wanted him to talk about the tunnel work he'd done in Canada. There were certain similarities in the method they proposed to use for the new extension.

Building bridges and viaducts on the West Highland Line had been a remarkable feat of engineering, but it was made possible because the stone used came from the actual railway site itself. No such stone existed for the extension.

It was while in Canada that Shaun had learned about the use of concrete and how it could affect future building. And his experience of new tunnelling methods would prove invaluable. That was all very well, he mused now, but how was he going to convince Rob Stewart? Shaun realised it was his Canadian experience which had clinched the foreman's job for him in preference to his old journeyman. Again, he took little pleasure from this knowledge.

In the old days, when they'd worked together in the tunnels, there had been several accidents. On one occasion Shaun himself had been trapped, and it was Rob Stewart who had dug him out with his bare hands.

Some accidents were caused by unsafe explosives, others by human failure. It was on this latter weakness that Shaun had been concentrating over the years. If new safety precautions were practised to the letter, he was convinced there would be fewer accidents.

He'd been aware of a strong wind blowing during the night, but was so tired after the long journey from Ireland that he'd fallen asleep during the worst of the storm. When he crossed to the window and leaned out over the roof next morning, he noticed activity down by the pier. Boats were getting ready to sail and men were scurrying about their decks.

As the clock downstairs chimed five, he realised he would be unable to fall asleep again. Pulling on thick corduroy trousers and a jumper, he decided to walk down to the pier. Gulls wheeled overhead as Shaun strode purposefully downhill. He had forgotten how bracing the wind could be here in the Highlands of Scotland, and shivered despite his thick clothing.

In Canada, winters were cold but dry, their summers gloriously hot. He'd been toying with the idea of sending for Rosa and of making their home there. He'd dreamed and planned for a life with Rosa and the child she was expecting. He had sent his wife to his home in Ireland to be cosseted by

44

his parents until the baby was due.

How was little Julie, he wondered. After Rosa's death, he'd spared little thought for that tiny mite, remembering only a thatch of black hair that reminded him painfully of his wife. His mam had promised to watch over the little one until he was ready to face that responsibility, and she'd made it easy for him to escape, with his excuse of important work in Scotland.

As Shaun reached the harbour wall he could see fishermen boarding their craft. There was an air of intense activity.

Two women in dark shawls passed where he stood.

'Oh, I do hope they find her,' one said to the other.

The second woman crossed herself.

'I believe it's young Will Stewart's boat, Catherine II. She's been missing for over twelve hours.'

He hurried after the woman. 'Did I hear you say a boat was missing, missus?' he asked.

'Yes, indeed. She was caught up in the bad weather last night and hasn't returned. The men are off to look for her right now,' one of them explained.

Shaun hurried back towards the sea-wall, a feeling of dread rising inside him. Will Stewart! He remembered how Rob used to talk about his only son, the one who'd let him down and left home.

A fishing boat was casting off directly below him, and Shaun leaned over the wall to get a better look. He thought he recognised one of the men aboard, a tall man with wide shoulders and hair that was now almost silver. As the man turned, looking directly up at him, Shaun felt sure it was Rob Stewart.

He lifted an arm to wave, but Rob Stewart gave no sign in return. Instead, he stared back at him dourly. There was no indication of the rapport they had once shared. So, Shaun mused, his suspicions had been correct – Rob blamed him for stepping into his shoes as Tunnel Engineer.

He watched now as a tall, red-haired fisherman gave orders from the wheelhouse and the sturdy boat sailed out of the harbour.

Beth had counted the hours until she could leave her room and help her mother in the kitchen below. 'I think Mhairi should stay here with us, Mum,' the girl said firmly. 'It wouldn't be right for her to return home in her condition and not knowing about Will.'

'You're right, Beth,' her mother agreed, 'but it will have to be Mhairi's own decision. She's a good lass and she has courage. Think of her tackling that journey from Mallaig. Will chose a fine girl for his wife.'

While they were all eating breakfast later, Mhairi surprised them once again. This morning she looked stronger, the shadows under her eyes almost gone. Beth noticed how her beautiful, glossy, dark hair had been brushed over her shoulders and that there was now a new, determined look in her eyes.

'I think I'll walk down to the harbour to hear if anything has–' she began.

'After you've finished your breakfast, lass,' Janet Stewart insisted.

'And I'm coming with you,' Beth added. 'Now are you sure you're up to it, Mhairi?'

The girl made a face. 'Beth, if I were back in Mallaig right now, I could be busy making breakfast for six men. I wonder how they're coping?'

'Let them get on with it,' Janet told her. 'It's high time you thought about yourself and your baby.'

The girl sighed. 'Perhaps you're right, Mrs Stewart.'

'I was just saying to Mother before you came down, I think you should stay here in the Fort, at least until the baby is born,' Beth put in. 'We'd be able to keep an eye on you here.'

Mhairi's eyes opened wide. 'Oh, I couldn't possibly, Beth,' she protested. 'I mean – they depend on me.'

'Pooh! You've allowed that to happen,

Mhairi. But you're married now, and Will and that baby you are carrying should be your only concerns from now on. Your father can engage a housekeeper to look after them.'

Mhairi looked unconvinced as she began to eat the plate of bacon and eggs Janet put in front of her. She ate ravenously. 'I've just realised, this is the first food I've eaten since lunch-time yesterday.'

Janet sniffed. 'You see what I mean. You've been neglecting yourself.'

Later, Beth and Mhairi walked together to the harbour. Ironically, the loch was like a mill-pond, with no sign of the winds that had whipped the surface into huge waves the night before.

'Oh, Beth, do you think...?'

The young nurse pressed the other girl's arm.

'Let's wait to hear what the fishermen have to say first,' she advised.

The harbour-master's office seemed quiet and there wasn't a single boat tied up outside. Everyone, it seemed, had gone out in search of Catherine II. Inside, they met Dan Crossan.

'No news yet, Mrs Stewart,' the harbour-master apologised as Mhairi made herself known, 'but you know what they say, no news is...'

'There's a boat coming in right now!' Beth

called from the doorway. 'I can see a head of steam out there at the entrance to the loch.'

The harbour-master rose quickly and came to the door, raising powerful binoculars to his eyes. 'Ay, you're right, miss. I can see her myself.'

In a voice that trembled, Mhairi asked, 'May I?'

Dan handed the glasses to Mhairi who trained them on the spot where Dan pointed. 'It's my brother Saul's boat,' she announced disappointedly after a few tense seconds, 'but he has nothing in tow.'

It was another half-hour before the fishing boat entered the harbour. By now the two young women were waiting on the pier, their hearts in their mouths. Rob Stewart could be seen standing with his back to the bridge. He caught sight of his daughter and began to wave frantically. As the boat came within hailing distance he cupped his mouth and began to shout.

'Will's safe, Beth! His boat has been sheltering off Rhum!'

Beth clasped her hands in delight and relief, and whirled round to share the good news with her sister-in-law. 'Isn't it wonderful, Mhairi?'

Mhairi, her face deathly pale, stared at her in despair. 'I don't understand!' she exclaimed. 'Why isn't Will with them? Why did they not tow the boat back to the Fort? I'm sure there's something wrong!'

'You mustn't jump to conclusions,' Beth soothed her. 'We'd better wait and ask Father.'

When Rob Stewart joined the two girls on the pier, he was full of news. Catherine II was aground, he explained, in a small, sandy bay and could not be moved until high tide. It had taken a lot of skill for Will to anchor her there for, as Saul mentioned earlier, he had had to rely on sail after the engine broke down.

'Then,' Rob continued, 'Will decided he might as well use the time working on the engine. He seems to think he can get her ready in time to back off under her own steam. Everyone's saying that was a good bit of seamanship, Mhairi,' he finished with quiet pride in his voice.

Saul McCallum came to stand by his sister's side. 'Will's all right, Mhairi,' he reassured her gently. 'He sends his love and told me to tell you that you've to stay with the Stewarts until he returns to the Fort. He asked me to make you promise!'

Colour was beginning to return to Mhairi's cheeks. 'Beth and Mrs Stewart have already offered me hospitality,' she explained, 'but how will you all manage back home, Saul?'

Her brother shrugged. 'It will do Father good to see just how much you did for us,

Mhairi. You just stay with Will's folk, I'll deal with Father.'

Mhairi relaxed almost visibly, and instead of the distraught young woman who had appeared at the Stewarts' cottage the previous night, Beth could see the vibrant, beautiful girl who had captivated her brother.

Now, she heard Mhairi chuckle and say, 'I'd like to be a fly on the wall when you do that, Saul!'

Beth hadn't stopped chattering since Alec Buller called at the cottage for her. By the time they reached the hotel where they were to attend a dinner, she had brought the young surgeon up to date with all her news.

'And do you think your brother will manage to get his boat afloat, Beth?'

The young nurse smiled. 'I'm sure he will. Anyway, even if he doesn't manage to salvage the boat, thank goodness he'll be all right with other boats standing by to rescue him.'

The hotel entrance looked very grand with tubs of plants in the vestibule. A frock-coated doorman examined their tickets.

'Ah yes, Doctor. Your table is right down at the front. You should be able to hear the speakers.'

Alec pretended to wince. 'Speakers, Beth? I hope we're not in for a long night,' he murmured.

As the young couple took their places, they noticed several frock-coated gentlemen at the top table. They looked very important, as did a splendid-looking lady seated beside the Chairman.

Lady Cameron of Locheil, who had cut the first sod in a field at Corpach five years before when the Mallaig extension was first suggested, had returned to celebrate its final approval after years of political disputes. The new Act specified the line should be completed by July 1902, five and a half years in which to build forty miles of track.

After a sumptuous banquet, it was time for the speeches. Alec made a face as the Chairman stood up to introduce the first speaker.

Unlike Alec, Beth found the speeches more interesting than she'd imagined.

When the new contractor, McAlpine, known amongst civil engineering circles as 'Concrete Bob,' was called upon to speak, she was enthralled by his enthusiasm. He spoke of the difficulties lying ahead, and the fact that the rock available on the extension could not be used to build bridges. This was why he proposed to use concrete. The tunnelling, too, would be more difficult, but they were lucky to have an expert in this field to help.

Beth suddenly noticed a man at the top table who, until now, had his back to her, but when the contractor called upon him to take the stage, her jaw dropped...

'We have with us tonight a young man who comes to us all the way from Canada. We are lucky to have captured his services. This is a man who has made safety practices in tunnelling his special aim in life.' Concrete Bob went on. 'Ladies and gentlemen, I'd like you to give a warm welcome to Shaun Nolan.'

'Beth,' Alec Buller whispered, 'you'd think you'd seen a ghost. What's the matter?'

But she felt too upset to speak. Here he was, the man who had treated her own father so abominably, being fêted and honoured by the Chairman of the railway board. As the audience clapped enthusiastically, she sat with both hands in her lap, her eyes not leaving the man's face for one moment as he stood on the raised dais.

Yes, it was Shaun Nolan all right. When he had come for his medical examination to the hospital, he had looked much the same as the other workers. Tonight, he looked different in his splendid evening suit and his hair slicked back. The youth who once lived under her father's roof was now a confident, mature man.

Reunions

Despite her distrust, Beth Stewart found herself listening to Shaun Nolan's voice with its lilting, Irish note, an accent which had not quite disappeared despite his years of travelling abroad.

Just once, she imagined his glance fell upon her, and his confident voice faltered. Beth watched him straighten his shoulders and begin to talk again, but she noticed how his gaze kept returning to where she sat. So, she thought with satisfaction, you do have a conscience after all, Shaun Nolan.

'That fellow spoke a lot of sense. Don't you agree, Beth?'

Beth and Alec were standing in the hotel vestibule, and Alec had just returned from the cloakroom with her woollen cape.

'He had a good tutor,' she told him grimly.

The doctor gazed down with some amusement at his small companion. 'My, something has ruffled your feathers!'

As he spoke, he could not help noticing how attractive she looked. Beth had chosen a blue, velvet dress with a tight-fitting bodice which accentuated her neat figure, and a simple string of pearls was her only jewellery. He had become used to seeing Beth Stewart in a crisp, cotton uniform. Tonight, her cheeks glowed and her dark eyes glittered.

Alec placed his hands upon her shoulders and leaned towards her, and it was at this moment that a tall, dark-haired man came hurrying towards the couple. Beth, catching sight of Shaun Nolan, felt panic rising within her. She gazed up at her companion then whispered something to him. For one moment the doctor seemed slightly surprised. He wondered if he had heard correctly.

'Kiss me, Alec,' she repeated urgently.

The tall Irishman halted in his tracks as he watched the couple embrace. He stood watching for several moments, his eyes narrowing, then with a shrug of his wide shoulders, he turned and made his way in the opposite direction.

Alec and Beth walked arm in arm along the towpath, the young doctor gazing down affectionately at his petite companion. She frequently surprised him, but tonight she'd astonished him.

He'd felt attracted towards the pretty young nurse from the moment he arrived in Fort William but, until tonight, she'd always kept him at a distance even when off duty.

Beth, aware of other staff at the infirmary watching her and Alec, seemed determined to give no cause for gossip.

The young couple reached a spot beside the loch where a willow tree gave them seclusion. With growing confidence, Alec caught Beth in his arms and pulled her towards him. For a moment, he thought he saw panic in her eyes.

'Please, Alec, not now,' she pleaded.

'Why not, Beth?' he demanded. 'You'd no such scruples up at the hotel, with a hundred folk milling around us!'

She turned her head away to hide her guilty expression. 'I know, and I'm sorry, Alec. That was unforgivable of me,' she whispered miserably.

'It didn't worry me!' he retorted. 'I've been longing to kiss you for weeks. I was just waiting for an invitation, and pardon me, Beth, I thought I received it tonight!' Placing a hand under her chin, he forced her to meet his gaze. 'Tell me I wasn't dreaming that the girl I held in my arms half an hour ago was warm and real and loving,' he urged more gently.

His lips met hers once more. This time she didn't resist but he could feel her lack of response. He released her immediately. 'What have I done to break the spell, Beth? What's wrong?'

She turned away almost guiltily. 'You did nothing at all, Alec. It was my fault, acting on impulse.'

'Nothing wrong with acting on impulse, my dear,' he assured her. 'It's usually when we show our true feelings.'

She still wouldn't look him in the eye, and the young doctor suddenly remembered something with a flash of intuition.

'Did that kiss have anything to do with a certain Irishman I saw approaching us at the hotel?' he demanded.

The startled look on her face told Alec his words had struck home. He felt his heart sink in bitter disappointment. They stood in silence for several moments before Alec said coldly, 'I don't much care for being "used", Beth, no matter how enjoyable the experience.'

She knew what he said was justified, and felt her face flush with shame. 'I really am sorry, Alec, but I couldn't think of any other way of putting him off. I just couldn't bear to speak to him after the way he treated my father,' she explained in a voice that shook.

Alec Buller took a deep breath. 'Perhaps I should see you home now.'

Beth turned towards him. 'I've hurt you enough. I can walk home by myself, Alec, I'm so sorry. I should never have—'

'That goes without saying,' he broke in, 'but I'll escort you home nevertheless. There are lots of strangers in Fort William with all these railway workers. Who knows what danger you could be in!'

She realised he was taunting her and that she deserved his scorn. Now she had lost the respect of someone she'd always admired.

They reached the cutting which led up to the Stewarts' cottage, and Alec once more laid a hand on Beth's arm.

She drew back instinctively.

'It's quite all right,' he told her icily. 'I've no intention of forcing my attentions on you. I just wanted to discuss something that's been on my mind for several weeks.'

Beth looked up at him, and a pang went through her for having caused this decent man such humiliation.

'It's just possible I may be leaving the infirmary, Beth,' he went on.

The girl gasped. 'Leaving, Alec? But why? Have I–'

His laugh sounded mirthless. 'Please don't flatter yourself, Beth. It has nothing to do with that little charade back in the hotel. There just happens to be a war taking place at this very moment. Haven't you read the posters at the infirmary? The government has been calling out for volunteers. Field surgeons are at a premium, I believe.'

'You mean the fighting in South Africa with the Boers?'

Alec nodded.

'But surely that has nothing to do with

us?' Beth asked, puzzled.

'No, Beth, that's where you're wrong,' the young doctor argued. 'Doctors have an obligation, and so do nurses. Have you forgotten Florence Nightingale and her efforts in the Crimea?'

She still didn't really understand what he was trying to say to her. Alec going off to take part in a war thousands of miles away? Surely he could not be serious? One look at his face told her otherwise, and, as the reality sank in, Beth felt sick at heart. She had allowed this man to come closer to her than anyone before.

'Oh, Alec, you haven't made up your mind to go, have you?'

He shook his head slowly. 'No! I haven't signed anything, if that's what you're asking, but I've been giving it serious thought. In any case, I don't intend to stay in this backwater for ever.'

'Good-night, Alec,' Beth said quietly. 'It's rather late. We'll talk about this some other time.' She hurried up the slope towards her parents' cottage, resisting the temptation to look back.

After the banquet was over and Shaun Nolan had said goodbye to his railway superiors, he decided to visit one of the town's several inns in the hope of meeting up with some of his countrymen.

The one he finally chose seemed patronised both by fishermen and railwaymen. Shaun could not help giving a wry smile when he saw there still seemed to be rivalry between the two work forces. Fishermen and railway builders invariably kept themselves strictly separated.

Shaun chose a seat at an empty table and listened to a conversation drifting towards him. It was mainly about the fishing boat, Catherine II, and the search for her amongst outlying islands.

Shaun felt rather lonely, for word had already got out about his promotion and the railwaymen appeared to be giving him a wide berth. They sat at the opposite end of the room from the fisherfolk. One man stood up and sidled towards Shaun. He recognised the man as a tunnel worker from the old days, but for a moment could not recall his name.

'Fearnan's the name,' the man supplied, hand outstretched. 'Didn't you work in the tunnels, back at the beginning of the West Highland Line? I think we were in the same team. Yes, I remember now, you were big Rob Stewart's blue-eyed boy. And what's this I hear about you stealing his job? Made up to foreman, eh? The boys won't like that.'

Realising the fellow was in an argumentative mood, Shaun decided not to encourage conversation. 'Go back to your mates before you say something you might regret, Fearnan,' he advised curtly. He finished his drink, but as he made his way back to his digs, he could hear the man's provocative laughter echoing in his ears.

He found it difficult to sleep after he returned to his room. He'd been on edge all evening, mainly because of the speech he'd had to make. He was primarily a practical man, more prepared for issuing orders to workers under his charge. Giving speeches was for politicians.

Then there had been that moment when he'd caught sight of Rob Stewart's daughter while speaking on the platform. That had shaken him. In the hotel vestibule later, he'd hurried over to have a word with her, hoping to arrange a meeting with her father.

Shaun felt fairly certain the girl had put on her show of affection for her escort for his benefit.

With a shrug, he turned away from the window and, crossing to the small dressing-table which his kindly landlady had provided, Shaun picked up a wooden-framed picture. He stared long and hard at the smiling face of his dead wife, Rosa.

One of a large family, Rosa was Spanish by birth, hailing from Seville where her folk were fruit growers.

Shaun had met her when his work took

him to Spain, and ever since then he'd counted himself a fortunate man.

Rosa gave up her birthright to travel with him to foreign lands. They'd lived in a covered wagon once, and in a tin hut in a shanty town, always moving to remote places whenever a railway was to be built. A girl used to sunshine, Rosa had not once complained about those inhospitable lands or the sheer physical hardship of their way of life.

It was only when she became pregnant that Shaun had decided she had put up with enough. The company he was working for were about to send him to Canada, another unknown country. Who knew what lay in store for them? He insisted upon Rosa travelling home to his family's farm in Ireland, where his mother would care for her.

As he lay on top of the bed clutching the photograph to him, Shaun Nolan came to a decision. He had to pick up the threads of his life. He would always cherish his memories of Rosa, but she wouldn't want him to grieve for ever. He'd been given an important job to do, and was responsible for the men who obeyed his orders. He was going to do the job well, he vowed silently, no matter what Rob Stewart or his flighty young daughter might think of him.

Beth threw herself into her work on

Monday morning. Another batch of rail workers had arrived off the first train and were due at the infirmary for their check-up. She was glad of the activity. It allowed her to work alongside Alec Buller with cool efficiency.

They'd reverted to their brisk working partnership. If, at times, his voice sounded curt, she was prepared to accept this.

'These files from Friday, Staff Nurse Stewart!' he called impatiently.

She looked up from her desk.

The doctor was holding out a bunch of grey folders to her. 'I notice you have not cross-checked the men's next of kin yet?'

'If you remember, Doctor,' she replied steadily, 'our last patient left just before the shift ended. You'll find all my notes at the back.'

She imagined the doctor's face reddened for a second, then he turned away. Beth could feel unbidden tears prick her eyelashes. Two junior nurses had been within ear-shot, and Beth could sense their curiosity. Quickly, she bent her head and returned to her work.

'Next of kin' lists were to be transferred into a hard-backed book after each man filled in a form setting out the information required. Railway workers came from great distances and, in case of accidents, the authorities demanded a list of the workers' families and where dependants might be contacted.

After the last man left, there was a quiet spell. Normally, Beth would have slipped into Alec's surgery to have a chat, but not today. She pulled the next-of-kin book towards her and began to turn pages. Her forefinger trapped the page bearing the initial 'N,' then travelled down the list until it reached 'Nolan, Shaun, aged twenty-seven. Marital status, widower.'

Beth closed the book sharply, aware of a constriction in her chest. For some reason, she discovered she was trembling.

'Pull yourself together,' she chided herself mentally. 'It's a long time since Shaun Nolan was part of your family.'

When the shift ended, Beth was glad to make her way home. Tonight, she did not wait to speak to Alec, or to confer about notes. Nor was she going to give him the opportunity to offer to walk part of the road home with her, as he usually did.

He had not spoken to her all day, other than on business. Beth preferred it that way, but as she strode into the night, she discovered she was feeling nervous and alone.

Only the thought of seeing Will again, of chatting with Mhairi and catching up on family news, lifted her spirits.

A full moon lit the way for Catherine II as

she slipped into Fort William that evening. To Will Stewart's surprise, several fishermen appeared on the harbour wall to give the crew a rousing cheer. Embarrassed, the bedraggled skipper raised a hand to return their salute.

His two-man crew scurried about the deck, tying up and securing hatches. Will Stewart leapt ashore and made his way up to the harbour-master's office.

'Well done, Stewart,' Dan Crossan congratulated him. Having heard of the fishing boat's imminent arrival, the harbour-master had waited to see her berthing. 'I hear you did a fine job out there.'

'It wasn't so tricky as it seemed,' Will admitted, reddening at the words of praise. 'You know, I never thought I would spare a kind word for my father-in-law. Dan, I've done nothing but complain about storing those wretched sails, but I wouldn't have stood a chance if it hadn't been for them last night. The rest was easy.'

'That's not what I heard,' a quiet voice broke in, and suddenly a shadowy figure came towards him from the harbour-master's fire.

'Father?' Will said tentatively.

Rob Stewart crossed the small office and threw his arms around his son.

'Och, lad, I'm sorry we quarrelled. I've been really worried about you. Can we let bygones be bygones?'

Father and son stood, each waiting for the other to speak. Rob was aware that Will had left his house a boy and was now a man, while Will knew how much this apology had cost his father.

'And I'm sorry about the wedding, Father. I mean–'

'Say no more, Will. I've met Mhairi and she's a fine lass.'

His son's drawn expression began to relax and he smiled. 'Oh, she's all that, Father. I couldn't believe it when Saul told me that she'd cadged a lift from him and set out to find me in her condition. I should have known, though. Mhairi's never lacked courage,' he finished with pride.

Rob was glad to hear his son's words, to know he had a good marriage.

Then the smile disappeared from Will's face. 'How is Mhairi, Father? That journey to the Fort must have taken a lot out of her in her...'

The older man nodded. 'Ay, the lass looked all in when she arrived, soaked to the skin and ready to drop, but your mother and wee Beth have been cosseting her since she arrived. She's looking much better now. You'll come up to the house and see for yourself?' he prompted.

Will looked embarrassed. 'It's been a long time,' he began.

Rob Stewart clapped his son on the shoulder. 'Ay, lad, it has that – and it's time to put things right. Your mother will be glad to see you.'

Beth paused to look up at the full moon, the indigo sky and the ridge of dark mountains. There was not a cloud in sight. She revelled in the quiet beauty of the night. She had reached a path which was fringed on either side by trees, which cast eerie shadows on the moonlit track. Normally, the walk home from the infirmary was a pleasant one. Tonight, for some reason, she felt strangely apprehensive.

By now she'd reached the viaduct, a tall, stone archway barring her path, but once around it, she would be able to see the banking and the short cut to the Stewart cottage.

It was as she stepped into the shadow of the stone pillars that the man appeared in front of her.

She heard a low chuckle which sent an icy shiver through her, then her arms were pinned behind her.

'Aren't you out late tonight?' the man sneered.

Beth opened her mouth to scream, but a coarse hand clamped down over her lips. Oh, Alec, she thought in panic, where are you tonight when I really need your help? As she sent up her silent plea for help, Beth became aware of a tall figure bearing down upon them. Her attacker's grasp on her slackened, and he was sent sprawling on the grass.

'I know you, Fearnan!' Shaun Nolan thrust his face close to the cowering man. 'I give you until first thing tomorrow to get on a train and go back to where you came from. There will be no work on the tunnels for you!'

Beth was standing with her back pressed against the wall, trembling, when the Irishman came to stand in front of her.

'Are you all right?' he asked anxiously. 'He didn't hurt you, did he?'

She shook her head, unwilling to put her thoughts into words. He picked up her cap from where it had fallen to the ground in the struggle.

'I shouldn't have let that rascal go!' Shaun exclaimed. 'I'll go and have a word with the constabulary if you like.'

'No, no,' Beth pleaded. 'So long as he leaves town, I don't want to make any fuss.'

'He'll leave, you can be sure of that,' he promised. 'I'll be at the station to see to it. Now, if you have no objection, I'll walk the rest of the way home with you.'

Beth didn't argue, feeling as if all the strength had drained out of her. She was still trembling and, noting this, the tall Irishman took off his jacket and began to wrap it about her. 'Here, this will help to make you warm. You've had a bad fright, lass.'

She nodded, unable to speak. As they reached the hill, and began to climb, she stole a glance at his face. This was not the Shaun Nolan she remembered from old, the youth who had played games with her in the kitchen, who had hoisted her on to his shoulders and taken her on to the moors to watch for eagles.

He looked older than his years. There were already traces of silver at his temples, and his skin, tanned from years of working abroad, had a network of wrinkles around his eyes.

'I hope this is not going to make you feel nervous about walking home from your work, Beth. Perhaps you should ask someone to meet you in future,' he suggested tentatively.

She was glad of the darkness hiding the flush on her cheeks as she thought of Alec and how often he'd escorted her home.

'And please don't judge the rest of the railway's casual workers by Fearnan. There's always one bad apple in the barrel,' he went on.

They reached the cottage gate, and Shaun leaned forward to release the latch. She turned to thank him for all he'd done, but he placed a finger to his lips. 'There's no need, Beth. I couldn't settle tonight. Now I'm glad I came out for a stroll...'

She shuddered as she realised how very differently the night could have ended.

'Perhaps you'd care to come in for a minute, Shaun,' Beth invited. 'I'd like to tell my parents how you came to my rescue back there.'

'No need,' he assured her briskly. 'I do intend to speak to your father, Beth, but it will keep a little longer. I don't believe this is the proper time. I heard earlier that your brother's boat was back safe and sound. There'll be a family reunion going on in there, so don't let me keep you.'

Shaun Nolan seemed very well informed, Beth thought, as she moved down the path. She could hear the sound of his heels on the flagstones, and turning, watched him going back the way they'd come. For some reason, Beth imagined there was a forlorn droop to his wide shoulders, then she remembered the information she had gleaned from her 'next of kin' book, information regarded as strictly confidential which could not be divulged to anyone, even her own family.

She pushed open the door of the cottage and immediately heard the swell of excited voices; Will talking quickly as he attempted to catch up with years of absence, and Mhairi's soft laughter as she joined in the conversation.

Beth closed the door softly and crept upstairs to her bedroom. Her cape was muddied but she would clean it up before going to work tomorrow.

A glance at her face in the mirror, however, told her that she had been right in coming upstairs before facing her family. She looked dreadful. Her cheeks, normally so rosy, looked deathly pale and her eyes spoke of her recent ordeal. If she let her family see her like this, they would immediately guess something serious had happened.

She remembered one of her mother's old tricks. Janet Stewart was always being told how pale she looked, and Beth was for ever pleading with her to have her blood checked. Her mother's answer was to nip her cheeks between forefinger and thumb to bring the colour back.

Beth did this now and studied the effect. She slipped into a blouse and put on the cardigan which Mhairi had knitted as her birthday present, then pulled on an oatmeal-coloured skirt taken from the wardrobe. As she glanced at her reflection in the mirror, she knew that no matter what trouble the Irishman had caused her father, she would be eternally grateful for his brave intervention. Surely his action deserved some recognition?

Carefully, Beth brushed her hair down

over her shoulders, and decided at last that she was showing no sign of her traumatic experience.

After all, she reminded herself, tonight was Will's night. She was determined the reunion should be a happy affair.

Rob Stewart was standing with his back to a roaring fire as Beth came quietly downstairs. It had been a long time since she'd seen her father looking so cheerful. For weeks, he had been fretting over his future with the railway company.

Now, with the safe return of his son, all earlier troubles had been pushed into the background. Turning, he caught sight of her. 'A busy night, lass? You look fair worn out.'

Beth, attempting to hide the turmoil that still raged inside her, realised all eyes were upon her. Her hands were shaking, and she clenched them tightly. It was the sight of her family looking so happy together that was proving too much.

Her father strode across the room and drew her towards the warmth. 'Janet, is there some cocoa left in that jug? Our wee Beth looks as if she could do with a cup.'

Beth smiled at the familiar gesture as he hooked both thumbs around his braces. 'Isn't this grand, lass, us being a proper family again? It calls for a celebration!'

Beth smiled wryly. Father had surely forgotten that it was his own intolerance which had kept Will from visiting the family home before now.

Mhairi, sharing the window-seat with her husband, rose to join her on the settee. 'Are you all right, Beth?' her sister-in-law whispered urgently.

'Of course,' the other girl replied instantly. 'It's just as Father says – I've had a busy shift at the infirmary.' Beth blushed as she lied, yet why should she spoil this important reunion by revealing she'd been attacked?

Try as she could, however, Beth was unable to throw off the memory of what had happened at the viaduct, and she shuddered involuntarily as she remembered her assailant's menacing eyes.

How could she ever feel anything but gratitude towards Shaun Nolan now? Yet because of his so-called betrayal, he was being considered their family's arch-enemy.

Beth felt unable to relax as family conversation floated around the cosy living-room. She wished she was upstairs again in her own bedroom, safe with her thoughts and hidden from family scrutiny. It was impossible, of course, for there were years of catching up to be done. The name Fergus McCallum seemed to feature frequently.

'Your father-in-law must be really hard,'

Beth heard her mother say to Will. 'Fancy treating Mhairi like that!'

'Fishing's not an easy life, Mrs Stewart,' Mhairi replied defensively. 'I don't suppose Father could ever change his ways. When my mother was alive, he used to work every hour God sent. Now, he's hung up his sea-boots, and is stuck at home with nothing to do all day but order us about.'

'Ay,' Will confirmed, 'he does that all right. I wonder what he'll have to say when he hears about Catherine II? I'm afraid she won't be fit to trawl for some time now.'

Beth gazed across at her brother. Everyone had feared the worst for this young skipper, but now he was looking very fit indeed, despite his long ordeal. The traces of silver at his temples gave her brother a distinguished look despite his weather-beaten skin.

'And what do you have to say, Beth, about your father's decision?'

Startled, Beth realised her mother was addressing her. Despite the relaxed atmosphere in the room, Janet Stewart appeared tense.

'Father's decision? I don't know what you mean.'

Her mother bit her lip. 'Och, sorry, lass, I forgot you've just arrived home. It's this business about the tunnel foreman's job. The Company has offered your father the

74

assistant foreman's job. Would you believe it! He's going to be answerable to that young upstart – Nolan!'

This was the moment Beth had been dreading, realising she was going to be dragged into taking sides. Strangely enough, it was her father who came to her aid.

'Janet!' Rob rounded on his wife. 'For one thing, the lad's not a boy any longer. He's seen a lot of the world since he lodged in our attic. As a matter of fact, word's going round that he's become very experienced through his travels. Did you know he's worked all over Canada and many other places besides?'

'Humph!' Janet flounced back to her sink and began to rattle cups. 'You know what they say about rolling stones, Rob. They gather no moss – just pick up a bit of polish – all I have to say is, he's got a colossal nerve. Shaun Nolan had better not show face in this house again.'

'Mother says you've come to a decision?' Beth prompted anxiously. She watched her father's face as varying emotions flitted across it.

'Ay, lass. Your mother here thinks I'm eating humble pie, but I've said I'll take the job,' Rob Stewart said quietly. 'I haven't waited all these years just to be left out on the extension now that it's finally been approved.'

Beth's heart went out to him. Her father was a proud man, and his decision to settle for second-best could not have come easily.

'Anyway, enough of railway talk, Beth,' Rob continued. 'What do you think of Will? Brought that fishing boat of his to the Fort with just a few scrapes from where she grounded.'

Beth looked across at Will, but he seemed embarrassed by this praise from his father.

'It was tricky, I'll give you that, but in a tight corner, any skipper worth his salt could have managed it,' he assured his family.

It occurred to Beth that she was seeing Will and Mhairi together for the first time. She was aware of something close to envy. Their life together could not have been easy, yet it was obvious for anyone to see that they were deeply in love. Will had come to stand behind his wife's chair. He laid his hands on her shoulders and Mhairi, in turn, looked up at him and smiled.

'Now listen, everyone.' Janet Stewart spoke with quiet authority. 'This chatting is all very fine, but some of us have to work in the morning.

'Just look at you, Beth. You're ready to drop. I hate those double shifts you've been working lately. Is there no sign of that Sister Baxter coming back?'

Beth felt a sense of relief. Her mother

seemed to have taken it for granted that her drained appearance was due to overwork. Somehow she'd got through the evening without giving herself away.

'Come Here And Be Kissed'

Mornings were always hectic at the infirmary. Beth worked for four hours, then after a break of two, she would be back on duty. Because of the absence on sick leave of the Duty Sister, she'd been required to work double shifts.

This morning, she was needed in Theatre to assist surgery.

All morning she'd been too busy to think about herself, and had found herself assisting Alec Buller. She saw the young doctor at his very best professionally. Beth had always admired his skill in Theatre, the sureness of his hands as he operated.

It was as she watched him work that Beth remembered what he'd said to her about not wanting to spend the rest of his life in this backwater...

Perhaps there was a grain of truth in Alec's words after all? They had often discussed the lack of facilities in the local infirmary, which had been formed originally as a cottage hospital to serve Fort William when it had been a straggling little town.

Alec Buller had trained in a large, city hospital where major surgery had taken place. Here, he was hampered by the lack of equipment, and forced to send the most serious cases to city hospitals, even although he was perfectly capable of performing those operations. As his nursing assistant, Beth had realised early on that they worked well together, but in her heart she was aware he was meant for greater things.

After surgery was completed, they were both glad to go outside. The sun was shining through the latticed windows of the ward as they passed through. Past animosity appeared to have been forgotten as Alec glanced at his watch. 'Come on, let's go and eat,' he said.

Beth began to relax. Alec Buller was not known to bear a grudge, and their gruelling day in theatre had put petty differences into perspective. As they walked downhill towards the town, she tried to match his energetic strides. 'Slow down, for goodness' sake,' she pleaded.

Alec stopped and gazed at her with some amusement.

'You're so small, Beth Stewart, yet all the time I've known you, you've been able to hold your own.'

'Must be my Stewart blood!' she retorted.

'We're renowned for being fighters.'

Catching hold of her hand, he tucked it into the crook of his arm, and slowed his steps to accommodate hers.

Since they had been seeing one another when off-duty, Alec and Beth had found their special meeting place, a small restaurant tucked down a side street and far away from hospital gossip.

They found a vacant seat by the window, which overlooked the harbour, and a rosy-faced waitress took their order.

After work, Beth had intended to speak to Matron about her sister-in-law. Instead, she found herself pouring out her concern to the young doctor. She explained about Mhairi's dash from Mallaig despite the imminent birth of her child. Alec listened carefully, then agreed that Beth had given sound advice. It was imperative, he said, that Mhairi remain in Fort William until after the delivery of her baby. To Beth's relief, Alec said he would arrange a check-up for Mhairi.

There was still some time before they were due back on duty, and Alec suggested they might walk down to the harbour.

'The wind off the sea will blow away the cobwebs,' he said, smiling.

Today, he sounded almost carefree, and when he took her hand inside his once more, Beth felt at ease with the world.

Suddenly they were both stopped in their tracks. They'd reached the dry-dock where Catherine II was now high and dry. The fishing boat looked a sorry sight with large scars across her paintwork. Beth looked at the ragged sails, awaiting repairs, the sails which had saved the boat – and its crew's lives. She turned and looked tearfully at Alec.

'This puts trivialities like ours into perspective, doesn't it?'

He squeezed her hand. 'Indeed it does, Beth. Forgive me for being so stupid the other night. I suppose I was jealous when I saw you and that Irishman. By the way, did you ever discover what the fellow was after?'

For a moment Beth remained silent. Surely it was time to tell Alec about the attack on her last night and how Shaun Nolan had come to her rescue? Yet, she couldn't bear to destroy the peace and tranquillity which had just returned to their relationship.

'I suppose it was just to apologise about his getting that job Father was after.' She shrugged. 'Anyway, it's settled now. Father has been appointed Assistant Foreman instead.'

The young doctor raised an eyebrow but made no comment. He looked fondly at the petite young nurse standing alongside him.

They had reached the cover of a shed which was used for storing lobster creels. Impulsively he drew her towards him.

'If it's any comfort to you, Beth, I don't really dislike this area. That was just me letting off steam last night. On a day like this, when the sun is shining and the loch is as calm as can be, the Fort has a lot to offer, not least when I'm with a certain young staff nurse,' he told her.

Then Alec turned serious. 'Beth, I suppose I'd better tell you something I heard this morning,' he began. 'Sister Baxter is coming back to work next week. You remember Matron implied she might retire on health grounds? Well, it seems Sister has made a good recovery. How do you feel about it?'

The news came as quite a shock and the disappointment showed in Beth's face. She tried to give him an honest reply. 'I can't say I'll miss the extra shifts, Alec, but I have to confess I enjoyed the responsibility. I'll certainly miss working closely with you…'

When he did not speak, she looked up and was surprised to see him smiling.

'I thought you might say that, Beth. I truly believed your post at the infirmary would be made permanent. After all, you have been filling in for Sister for months. As a matter of fact, when I was speaking to Matron, I did mention the possibility.'

'Thanks anyway, Alec – for speaking up

for me, I mean,' Beth said, swallowing hard.

'There's no need to thank me, Beth. Matron says you've been more than ready for promotion for a long while. Don't give up hope,' he urged. 'You never know what's on the cards.'

The girl felt slightly taken aback by the surgeon's calm acceptance of the situation, but when he put his arms around her she did not resist. She was feeling vulnerable and in need of solace, and when his lips met hers, she responded willingly.

They spent the rest of their free time walking by the loch. The wind from the water had brought colour back to Beth's cheeks, and the disappointment regarding the end of her promoted post began to recede. For months now she had been doing the work of Sister but without the formal recognition of that rank's authority.

What, she wondered, would the junior nurses have to say about her reversed status? She was well aware that there was always a certain amount of jealousy among the lower ranks when it came to promotion.

Mentally, Beth squared her shoulders. Problems came in many sizes and she felt sure she could handle any new ones.

The rest of the day's shift passed smoothly enough, until Beth was called to Matron's office. She checked that her cap was straight and smoothed her uniform before tapping on Matron's door.

The older woman smiled in welcome. 'Come in, Staff Nurse Stewart. I believe Doctor has told you about Sister Baxter?'

Beth nodded.

Matron was skimming through papers on her desk, then looked up. 'Well, of course, I have come to depend upon you greatly, as has Dr Buller. You've applied yourself well and it has been noted.

'You must understand, however, that Sister Baxter is a vastly-experienced nurse and would be greatly missed if she decided to retire. Still, one never knows what is round the corner, does one?'

As with Alec, Beth imagined there was a slightly-offhand tone in Matron's words and that the subject was being lightly dismissed. Once more she experienced disappointment. It was as if all her hard work had gone for nothing.

'Will that be all, Matron?'

'Yes, Staff Nurse. Carry on as usual.'

The rest of her duty period passed slowly, and Beth had ample time to get her thoughts in order and look on the positive side. Now that she was due some time off, she planned to make good use of it. She would get to know Mhairi better, she decided, and spend time with her brother, too.

What a difference a break would make. If she tried hard enough, surely she could forget the events of the past two days?

It was just as she was about to go off duty that Robert McAlpine arrived, and Beth and Alec were summoned to meet him in Matron's office.

He shook hands first with Alec, then Beth.

The contractor's visit to the infirmary was primarily to examine the medical records of his workers. He turned back to Alec.

'We are going to be working hard, Doctor, and I want to be sure the men we employ are fit for the job.'

Beth noticed two younger men hanging back as Concrete Bob spoke. He beckoned them across.

'These are my sons, Robert Junior and Malcolm. Robert here will be in full charge of construction, and Malcolm his assistant. While we're here, I'd be obliged if you would give the pair a check-up. After all, what's good for the workers...'

'But, Father!' The younger of the men turned crimson. 'Do we have to?'

'Indeed you do!' the older man retorted.

It emerged there was another reason for Robert McAlpine's visit to the infirmary.

'I would like to put you all in the picture,' he explained. 'This is going to be the biggest feat of engineering in Britain, and we, as a company, will be responsible for a lot of workmen.'

Beth was astounded to learn that over three and a half thousand navvies would eventually be working on the line, consisting of Irishmen, Lowland Scots, Highlanders and men from the islands who spoke only Gaelic.

Matron produced the sheaf of papers Beth had seen her working on earlier.

'Ah, Matron, you've brought the documents I requested.'

'Yes, Mr McAlpine. Dr Buller explained what you needed.'

Beth watched a strange look being exchanged between Alec and Matron, almost as if they were conspirators.

'I've come to pick all your brains,' Concrete Bob admitted cheerfully. 'You see, the Company have suggested that we set up a hospital for the camp alone, and at a more central point. It would just be for emergencies, you understand. Our men will be working in isolated spots all along the proposed extension, and it will not always be possible to get medical help quickly for them, should the need arise.

'I've been making some investigations and I've decided upon the old schoolhouse at Lochailort,' he continued. 'Of course, with the means at our disposal, it would have to be a rather modest affair. What was it you suggested, Doctor?'

Alec Buller answered immediately. 'I

thought perhaps eight beds, sir, a couple of nurses and, of course, a resident doctor in charge.'

'Mr McAlpine, I'd like Staff Nurse Stewart to be in charge of the nursing side,' he went on. 'That is, if she's agreeable?'

'Yes,' Matron broke in, 'we both feel Staff Nurse Stewart should be chosen. I should point out that she has been acting Sister in Charge here for several months and is highly qualified.'

Concrete Bob turned to Beth. 'So you are the young lady held in such high esteem?'

He laid a large map on the table and signalled that they study it closely.

'You see, it would be here, between Glenfinnan and Beasdale,' he said, pointing with a pencil. 'We propose to build one of our largest camps here, at Lochailort, and the old schoolhouse is the proposed site for the hospital, as I've already explained.

'What do you say, Staff Nurse Stewart? Would you consider coming on the company pay-roll and accepting the position of Nurse in Charge? Mind you, it would carry a fair bit of responsibility,' he warned.

She looked up confidently. 'I would be honoured to accept the post, sir,' she told Robert McAlpine.

The contractor turned to the surgeon now. 'And you, Doctor?'

Alec Buller was looking keenly at Beth.

'Yes, sir. I've been giving it a lot of thought since the offer was first made. I agree with you there will be a need for medical access closer to the line. I, too, will be looking forward to the move,' he declared.

It was decided that Alec and Beth would visit the site that weekend and inform Mr McAlpine of its requirements from the medical point of view.

Later, Alec walked Beth home.

'Why the big secret about Lochailort, Alec?' Beth asked. 'Why didn't you say?'

The doctor spread his hands. 'How could I, Beth?' he protested. 'I didn't know how I felt about it myself. In fact, we didn't hear about the proposal until last week. Both Matron and myself felt you would be ideal for the new position, but she insisted that I say nothing to you until McAlpine himself offered you the post. You are certain it's what you want, Beth?'

She nodded emphatically. 'The experience will be invaluable, and Matron says the posting will mean I'll be permanently established in my promoted ranking.'

As they walked on, Alec talked about their visitors. 'McAlpine seems to know what he's about, doesn't he? The men say he's a hard taskmaster, but doesn't spare himself.'

Beth nodded. 'I don't know if his sons would agree. They put up a fair bit of argument about having to be examined!'

The couple laughed as they recalled the event and the indignation of young Malcolm when told he would require to have his teeth seen to shortly.

As they reached the viaduct, Beth stopped in her tracks and clutched Alec's arm.

'What's wrong?' he said, seeing how frightened she looked.

'I'm sure I saw something,' she explained lamely. 'A figure standing over there, behind that tree.'

The young doctor stared at her. 'Beth, whatever's the matter? It's not like you to be so nervous.'

'A man jumped out at me last night, Alec. I thought I'd got over it... Perhaps this is just a reaction.'

'You mean someone tried to attack you here, Beth, and you told no-one?'

She looked down in distress.

'Beth! Tell me, where did you think you saw something?'

She pointed towards the clump of trees, and he strode towards the spot determinedly. 'Please be careful!' she called after him. As he neared the trees, a figure detached itself from them, and came to stand directly in front of Alec.

The man stared at Alec truculently.

'*You!*' the doctor shouted. 'So it was you skulking about here to frighten that poor girl again! Well, let's see how brave you are when you meet someone your own size!'

The man by the trees turned towards Beth.

'For goodness' sake, Beth! Tell him who I am!' Shaun Nolan called out.

Beth seemed frozen to the spot as Alec Buller sprang forward and the two men grappled.

'Stop it!' Beth shouted, as the two men struggled. 'You're both making a mistake!'

Alec swung around and Beth saw disbelief fill his eyes. 'What are you saying? Didn't a man attack you here last night? Just a minute ago, you were certain someone was hiding in the trees...'

Beth felt close to tears. 'Yes,' she agreed unsteadily. 'But it wasn't Shaun! He came to my rescue!'

The Irishman stood, arms folded, as Beth intervened.

'Why were you waiting here anyway, Shaun?' she went on to ask. 'I did see you behind those trees, didn't I?'

He looked slightly embarrassed.

'Well, if you must know, I wanted to make sure you were all right. And tell you you have nothing to fear from that lout, Fearnan. I personally saw him off on the train this morning,' he assured the girl. 'I was taking no chances that he'd try for work farther down the line. Anyway, I can see you're in capable hands, so I'll be on my way.'

He nodded to both of them. 'Good-night, Beth. You, too, Doctor.'

Lochailort was to be the largest campsite on the route of the Mallaig extension. Today, even at such an early stage of construction, there was a buzz of activity. Several huts had been set up to accommodate the workforce, each hut serving forty men. The early arrivals were the pick-and-shovel men, who would dig foundations, clear timber and cut swathes through the land where the line would be laid.

By five o'clock in the morning, the men were out of bed, washing in cold water from the mountain burns, then it was off to the main hut to prepare their own breakfasts. The ground around the camp was already churned into a sea of mud by iron wheels and hob-nailed boots.

Another ferry had just tied up at the pier, and two passengers stepped gingerly ashore. Beth Stewart shielded her eyes with both hands and looked in amazement at the sight before her. A large, wooded area was being cleared, and tree-trunks lay at odd angles on either side of the rough track. A group of workmen standing nearby gazed with interest at the new arrivals.

'What a hive of activity, Alec!' the girl

exclaimed. 'How on earth do they know where to start?'

'I'm glad we'll only be here to bandage up wounds,' he said with a chuckle.

They should have been met at the pier by young Mr Robert McAlpine. He was to escort them to the site of the proposed hospital, but he was nowhere to be seen. As they stood on the pier, a familiar figure detached itself from a group of workers and strolled across.

'We meet again, it would seem,' Shaun Nolan greeted Beth. The Irishman touched his forehead in a careless salute as he recognised Alec Buller. 'Good day to you, too, Doctor.'

'We were supposed to be met by Mr Robert McAlpine,' Alec told him.

Shaun smiled. 'He's away back to the Fort with his brother, to check on our steam compressors – they've been acting up. Anyway, I believe it's the schoolhouse you're after. The boss told me about your visit before he left. I promised him that I would take you there myself.' He stepped aside and motioned them to a large wagon loaded high with bags of cement.

With a frown, Alec handed Beth up on to the seat, then he too climbed up beside the driver. Shaun Nolan made do with a sack placed on top of the load. He gave a signal to the driver, and with a flick of the long whip the team of horses and the wagon moved slowly uphill.

Beth turned round to speak to the Irishman. 'Father told me last night about trouble with the new tunnel. He left hours before us this morning, and I foolishly thought we might meet him here. Going by the number of workers around, it would be like looking for a needle in a haystack!' She stopped, then added, 'Of course, you'll know all about that – since you're the foreman now.'

'I was talking to him just half an hour ago,' Shaun said. 'He hasn't changed much.' It seemed he was determined not to be goaded.

The heavily-laden wagon began to gain pace, and Beth felt as though every bone in her body was being jarred. She clung on to Alec's arm to stop herself from being thrown off her seat.

'Won't be long now,' their guide assured them. 'The old schoolhouse is just over the top of this hill.'

Beth noticed Shaun had risen to his feet and was balancing himself expertly on top of the load of cement, despite the crazy angle of the swaying vehicle. He pointed towards a dilapidated grey building which stood stark against the horizon.

As the wagon drew up alongside the building, Alec started to climb down, but, in doing so, brushed against one of the sacks of cement. White dust clung to his dark suit. As a professional man, he'd always been meticulous about his appearance, and with a look of distaste, he attempted to brush himself down. Then, as he turned to help Beth, Alec realised the Irishman had beaten him to it. With one sweep of his muscular arms, he'd scooped up Beth and landed her on the ground.

'We had our own hospitals on the camp-sites in Vancouver,' he explained conversationally. 'We usually built them with logs, so they could be dismantled and rebuilt as the gangs moved on.'

The disused schoolhouse turned out to be deceptively large, with several buildings and outhouses. Beth began to take a keener interest. 'I really think there are possibilities here, Alec, with some hard work.'

Alec stroked his chin. 'I daresay. This, for instance, could be Reception with a day clinic off.'

The two of them continued to discuss ways and means.

Shaun, leaning against a wall, listened to them enthuse. Now he straightened himself. 'Look, the pair of you seem to know what you're doing, so I'll leave you to get on with things. I'll hitch a ride back to the camp and try to track down the boss – Mr McAlpine.'

Beth had forgotten he was still with them.

'I'm sorry, Mr Nolan,' she apologised. 'We mustn't keep you from your work.'

'Not a bit of it,' he assured her. 'Everything has ground to a halt for the tunnellers right now. Would you believe the surveyors thought we might get by with only two tunnels on the extension! It's my guess they'll need a lot more than that before we're finished.'

'Indeed,' Alec Buller spoke curtly. 'Well, I'm sure you're right, Nolan. Thanks for getting us here, but, as you said, we'll be all right on our own now.'

The snub was intentional, and Shaun raised his eyebrows. 'In that case, I'll be off,' he declared. 'Good day to you.' He took a couple of strides then turned.

'Have you thought how you'll get back to the pier to catch the ferry? The ground would be very rough for this young lady, that is, if you intend to walk.'

Alec hadn't planned for this, and his cheeks reddened.

Shaun shrugged. 'You can do what the schoolmistress must have done in the old days – ring that bell in there.'

Beth and Alec stared in the direction Shaun pointed. A large bell was set in an alcove above the front door.

'Five pulls and we'll send up a trap for you, eh?' Shaun suggested.

Beth bit her lip as she watched him stride down the path.

'Did you have to be so rude to him, Alec? He didn't have to help us, you know.'

The doctor's face was still flushed, and now Beth watched his mouth tighten. 'Beth, I'm getting pretty sick of having that man's good deeds paraded. I don't intend to be grateful to him for the rest of my life!' he said irritably. 'In any case, why's he always around? I'm beginning to think he must have an ulterior motive.'

Beth took one look at his face and decided she would remain silent. After all, they were going to spend the rest of the day together. She had packed a lunch, and hoped there might be time to enjoy a picnic later.

They began to make a detailed inspection of the property.

When they entered the last of the upstairs rooms, she exclaimed in delight. 'Oh, Alec, come and see this!'

Beth was pointing to a magnificent view from a window. All around were mountains, and from their vantage point it was possible to look down over Lochailort.

'Yes,' Alec agreed quietly, 'it's a beautiful area. Pity it has to be spoilt.'

Beth turned on him indignantly. 'Spoilt? You mean by building a railway? Shame on you, Alec. This will not be just a tourist attraction, you know. It will be a lifeline for folk like my brother, Will – a means of getting fish to the markets on time.'

He studied her with some amusement. 'Your temper certainly lives up to that red hair.' He held out his arms. 'Come here and be kissed!'

Beth blushed. 'Someone could be watching,' she protested.

Alec threw back his head and laughed then pointed his finger. 'Look out there, Beth. There are only lochs and mountains. You're not afraid of me, surely, now that your fine Shaun Nolan has left us alone at last?'

'He's not my Shaun Nolan.'

'Prove it, then,' he challenged, putting his arms round her and bending his head. Shyly, Beth raised her lips to his.

Several times as they'd walked around the old schoolhouse, Alec had seemed on the verge of saying something. It was as they prepared to leave that he'd pointed to the little empty cottage standing near the main house.

'Nurses' quarters,' he'd suggested softly. 'Or perhaps more suitable for a married couple?'

She'd looked up questioningly.

'You must admit we make a good team,' he'd pointed out.

Was he teasing – or expecting a reply?

Beth had literally been saved by the bell.

Earlier, when their tour of inspection was complete, Alec had done as Shaun Nolan had suggested and rung the school bell. Now a horse-drawn cart approached them.

It was early evening when Alec and Beth arrived back at Fort William. After today's closeness, how could she ever maintain the necessary detachment in her working life? she asked herself.

The streets of the Fort were still thronged as the young couple left the pier. Beth asked if Alec wanted to come up to the house for a meal, but he shook his head.

'Some other time, Beth. I'd better get back to my digs. I have all these notes to write up, and some letters besides. I'll walk with you, though,' he told her.

She began to protest, but he placed a finger to her lips. 'No arguments, Beth, I insist.'

As soon as she opened the front door, Beth could see light streaming from their sitting-room, a room rarely used unless there were visitors. Amid the hum of familiar voices she became aware of a strong, resonant accent, one she'd never heard before.

Her observant eye also noticed a strange-looking walking-stick in the stand by the door, but as she entered the room, she was unprepared for the unusual vision in the corner. Sitting in an armchair was a very tall man. A snow-white beard reached down to his chest. In his hand he held a seaman's dark cap.

Janet Stewart, wearing a white apron and carrying a tray, seemed agitated. 'This is Mr McCallum, Beth,' she introduced quickly. 'Mhairi's father. He's come to pay us a visit.'

The man did not rise from his chair. Instead, he stared boldly at Beth.

'So you're the one who's been putting daft ideas into my daughter's head!' he accused. 'Mhairi's place is at home in Mallaig, where she belongs.'

Fergus McCallum was certainly living up to his reputation of being the unreasonable, arrogant father-in-law Will spoke about, but the man had not allowed for the maturity given to Beth by her nursing.

'And when, sir, did you become such an authority on what is good for a pregnant woman?' she retorted.

The fisherman's face was slowly flushing with temper. 'Her mother had all of our sons and Mhairi, too, at home, and with just a midwife in attendance. She came to no harm,' he growled.

Beth could hardly believe her ears. 'Mr McCallum,' she said with steel in her voice, 'Mhairi's life is not to follow the pattern of your wife's. I've spoken to the doctor. He's arranging her check-up and he will say where Mhairi has her baby. Until then, she stays here!'

Fergus McCallum turned to the head of the house. 'Stewart!' he roared. 'You allow your daughter to speak like this to me?'

Rob Stewart had spent his first working day up at the Lochailort site. His meeting with Shaun Nolan had fortunately been brief. The new foreman had become caught up in a difference of opinion with the management. They were having great difficulty with their steam-operated air compressors.

It had been a wasted day so far as Rob was concerned, for the bosses decided to return to Fort William. Then Shaun sent him back to the tunnel site, although no work could be undertaken.

Disheartened, he'd sailed home when his shift was complete, only to discover Fergus McCallum holding forth in his own parlour. Mhairi was in a flood of tears, and Will attempting to console her.

Until now, Rob had been unwilling to take sides in this family squabble, but now the futility of his day spilled over.

'I'd ask you, sir, to mind what you say about my family. Beth's a qualified nurse and knows what she's talking about. As for Mhairi, she can stay here just as long as she wants, and with my blessing. You can hire your own skivvy,' he finished.

Any moment now, Janet Stewart decided,

that old man was going to have apoplexy. She hurried across with her tray. 'Here, Mr McCallum, I think you should have some tea.' She thrust a cup of tea into his hands before he could refuse. 'The evening meal will be ready in a minute,' she went on.

Fergus was speechless. He stared down at the cup. Then threw back his head and laughed aloud.

'Well!' he exclaimed at last. 'Scolded by a chit of a girl, then her father tells me I'm a tyrant, and his wife has the nerve to offer me tea. I just don't believe it!'

'Does this mean I can stay?' Mhairi asked anxiously, deciding to strike while the iron was hot.

Her father eyed her. 'I suppose you'll do as you think fit, Miss. I can't beat a whole army of Stewarts!'

Before going to bed, he dropped another bombshell, asking Rob Stewart if he could stay with them for a few days. He wanted a good look at Catherine II to discover if the boat was worth salvaging.

Highland courtesy could not be denied. 'Why, of course, you're welcome, McCallum, if you don't mind using the boxroom.'

And so it was all settled and the old man yawned, indicating that it had been a long day.

'Both Well, I Trust?'

As Beth awoke the next morning and was about to jump out of bed, she remembered – today, she did not have to go into work.

'Time off in lieu,' Matron had called it, to make up for all those double shifts she had worked in Sister Baxter's absence.

Beth decided she would make the most of this extended leave. She would get to know her sister-in-law better in the time at her disposal. She was also determined that she would keep a professional eye on Mhairi's health at this late stage of her pregnancy.

Beth got up and poured water from a jug into its matching basin. She shivered as the cold water touched her skin. She would make a point of getting Mhairi on her own as soon as possible, she promised herself.

'What's this Mhairi's been telling me about these problems having her bairn? She never mentioned it to me when she was at home,' Fergus McCallum asked Beth later, as he sat at the kitchen table, eating a large bowl of porridge.

Beth, sitting opposite him, frowned. 'Did you ever ask your daughter how she was feeling?' she snapped. 'You surely must have noticed how exhausted she looked, having to run after your household of men.'

The fisherman looked away but he said no more.

Beth went on determinedly. 'Anyway, I'm thinking of taking her for a check-up this morning, since I'm not on official duty today.'

She caught the look of surprise on Mhairi's face and explained. 'There's a clinic this morning, Mhairi. I don't think you should put it off too long.'

After breakfast, she waited while Mhairi got ready, noting how swollen the other girl's ankles seemed.

Later, they walked with arms linked towards the viaduct. Mhairi needed to stop rather often in order to catch her breath, and Beth was beginning to develop a conscience about insisting on this check-up. After all, she could have called in the family doctor for an opinion, she thought guiltily.

Mhairi leaned against the wall and Beth waited, every now and then glancing over her shoulder. The viaduct was a place which made her feel uneasy nowadays.

'Are you all right, Mhairi?' she asked her companion anxiously.

'I'll be fine when I get my breath back,' Mhairi replied with a weary sigh. She straightened herself, rubbing her back.

Beth frowned. 'Perhaps it's not such a

good idea taking you to the clinic this morning. If you don't feel up to it, we could go back home,' she suggested.

'You did spring it on me unexpectedly,' Mhairi admitted, then turned to face the younger girl. 'I couldn't help wondering, Beth, if it was for my benefit, or to prove a point to Father?'

Beth found herself blushing. This sister-in-law of hers was shrewder than she thought.

'I don't know why you keep on defending him, Mhairi, after all the things I've heard about him,' she protested.

Her companion shrugged. 'We grew used to his ways, Beth. Anyway, Will had more to put up with than I did. Catherine II was Father's own boat – she's really close to his heart – but Will says she's only fit for the scrapyard these days.'

Beth shook her head. 'You two must have been saints to put up with him!'

Rather impatiently, Mhairi retorted. 'No, we were just being practical! While we were living under Father's roof, it was only courtesy to do what he wanted.'

'Then why didn't the pair of you leave long ago, for goodness' sake…' Beth began, before raising her hand to her mouth. 'What am I saying? There was nowhere else for you to go, was there?'

Mhairi looked at the ground without speaking.

'I see,' Beth went on slowly. 'Will couldn't come back to the Fort because of quarrelling with my father, so he had to depend on yours for a livelihood?'

'That's about the size of it, Beth. We both appear to have rather obstinate fathers,' she said with a wry smile.

'Poor lass.' Beth was about to put her arm round Mhairi's shoulders, but the other girl drew away.

'I'm sorry, Beth, but I must say this. You behaved rather intolerantly towards Father this morning,' she declared. 'He's an old man now, and has nothing left but his pride. Besides, I must tell you it wasn't all doom and gloom living in Mallaig. We had good times, too. Father is not nearly as black as he likes to paint himself, and my brothers are a cheery lot.'

Beth's eyes widened. How wrong she'd been to imagine Mhairi quiet and submissive. Her loyalty to her family was obviously deep-rooted.

It was Sister Baxter's first day back on duty, and after Beth had escorted Mhairi to the clinic and introduced her to the duty nurse, she decided to pop into out-patients for a chat with the senior nurse.

'How are you?' Beth asked anxiously.

'Never better,' Sister Baxter assured her.

Beth showed the older woman the notes she'd prepared when the railway men had their medicals.

Sister Baxter nodded. 'Yes, I've been hearing great things about you from Matron. What's this about you accepting a new posting?'

Beth had been longing to talk to someone about the proposed move to the camp hospital at Lochailort, and indeed the inspection carried out with Alec the previous day.

The sister proved an interested listener. 'Sounds exciting.' She sighed. 'Wish I were your age again, Beth. It's a wonderful challenge to be in at the start of something new. You'll have to live in, of course?'

Beth nodded ruefully. Her work at the infirmary had always proved demanding. But there had always been home to go back to once her shifts were over. Her new independence in the future could have its drawbacks.

'I'm not too happy about Mhairi,' Alec Buller said when at last Beth was able to corner him. 'You were right to bring her in. Her blood pressure is a bit high, and she tells me she's already had one miscarriage.'

Beth drew in her breath. 'I didn't know that, Alec. She never said anything to me.'

'She's a strong character, Beth, with a will of her own,' he soothed. 'You know, I would have made a house-call, Beth, if you had sent for me. I suggested we keep her in for a few days, but she seems determined to go home. Here's what I've decided to do.'

As Alec continued to adopt his most professional attitude, Beth wondered if it was possible to feel glad yet disappointed at the same time. This morning there seemed little sign of the rapport which had existed between them the day before at Lochailort.

'I'm sending Mhairi home by ambulance,' he told her.

Beth nodded. 'Then I'll go back with her.'

Alec's hand rested lightly on her shoulder. 'I've arranged for an attendant to go with her, Beth. I'd prefer if you stayed on here for a bit.'

When Beth glanced up, she was unable to interpret the look on Alec's face, but he seemed to be watching her closely.

She stood and watched as he supervised Mhairi's transfer to the ambulance.

'I'll see you soon, Mhairi,' she called, and her sister-in-law waved her arm.

'Don't hurry, Beth. I'm being very well looked after as you can see, and Dr Buller says he has some urgent business to discuss with you.'

'Urgent business?' Beth repeated as the ambulance doors were closed and the driver urged the horses to move. She turned and noticed Alec's heightened colour.

'We can discuss it just as easily over

lunch,' he said hastily. 'Wait here until I get my coat.'

Alec and Beth walked towards the waterfront and their favourite tearoom. Alec found a table in a little alcove where they could have complete privacy.

'Your notes on the old schoolhouse were splendid, Beth,' he began quietly. 'I've seen McAlpine and put our points to him. Everything seems to be working out quite well.'

So Alec had indeed taken her to lunch to talk business, Beth realised.

'From now on, I'm going to be extremely busy. There will be so much catching up to do, all those records to be transferred to the camp hospital. I'm afraid we won't be able to see very much of each other socially for a while. Things will be different at Lochailort. You understand what I'm trying to say, don't you?' he asked tentatively.

Beth nodded her head slowly, unable to trust herself to speak. A pleasant interlude – was that all yesterday meant to Alec?

Suddenly he leaned across the table and caught hold of both her hands.

'You have such capable hands, Beth. I think the two of us will make a fine partnership. Beth – I've something to ask you.'

She waited expectantly, her pulse quickening.

'I'm at a stage in my career when I should be thinking about the future,' he said seriously. 'I even thought for a while I might enlist in the Army as a surgeon, but I've decided against that for the time being. On the other hand, when the railway contract ends, I don't know what I'll do.'

Beth listened closely, her eyes trying to read his face.

'I'm twenty-eight, Beth. It's time I was putting down some roots, and I believe I have something to offer.'

'You're a splendid surgeon, Alec.'

He shook his head in impatience. 'I'm not talking about my prowess with the scalpel, Beth, I'm talking about us – you and me. I care a great deal about you and I think you feel something for me, too. When we move to Lochailort we're going to be thrown together...'

She waited for him to say more, but he seemed lost for words. The colour had risen in his face, and with sudden insight Beth realised that under his business-like exterior, Alec Buller was a shy man. Perhaps he thought that she might rebuff him.

Beth knew that she could have helped him now, encouraged him to ask her that most important question, yet something inside her held her back. When and if Alec Buller asked her to marry him, he must do so without promptings from her.

At Corpach, the first site on the new extension, Rob Stewart was organising a party of navvies.

'How goes it, Rob?'

He looked up and found Shaun Nolan standing on the embankment.

'Checking up on me already?' Rob said curtly.

The Irishman sighed, then signalled for him to follow him to the cabin out of earshot of the workmen.

'Now let's get one thing straight, Rob,' Shaun told the older man bluntly. 'We're going to be working closely together for a long time. Think of me what you must, but during working hours, let's call a truce.'

He held out his hand.

'All right, Nolan. That makes sense, I suppose.'

Solemnly they shook hands, but Shaun did not miss the older man's reluctance, nor the fact that he was being addressed as Nolan.

They spoke at length about mutual difficulties they were experiencing with drilling, and Shaun said he was worried about the use of explosive due to take place at the end of the week. 'We'd similar trouble in Canada. Hard rock just like this, Rob. There were several accidents caused by fragments ricocheting and wounding many of our tunnel men.'

'Yes,' Rob agreed, 'and I'm not too sure about these men we've been sent, either. Very few of them seem experienced.'

Shaun turned to look out of the hut window. The workers were a motley crew and no mistake – men who had travelled many miles, all of them hungry for work.

'They'll learn,' he said philosophically. 'Experience is a very good teacher. Wasn't that what you told me once?'

The two men stared at each other, remembering years gone by when their positions had been reversed.

A horn sounded for the end of the shift, and as Rob and Shaun left the hut men were beginning to crowd around a wood stove. Some of the more experienced washed their shovels in a nearby stream. They began to cook eggs and bacon on the shining blades. Tea was brewed in smoke-blackened cans, and the sounds of cheerful conversation filled the air.

Rob and Shaun smiled at each other for the first time.

'Just like the old days, Rob,' the younger man said. 'I remember you taught me that trick of cooking on the end of a shovel.'

One workman came away from the stove and sauntered across to where they stood. 'The lads tell me you saw Fearnan off the other day, Mr Nolan. They'd like to know why? He was a fair enough worker.'

Shaun's eyes flashed. 'Are you trying to tell me my job, Kelly?' he retorted. 'Just leave the hiring and firing to those whose job it is. Now get back to your cronies.'

'Something I should know about?' Rob probed.

'Not this time, Rob. Trust me.'

The older man was silent.

Just a moment ago Shaun had suggested they call a truce, but it seemed as if it was to be one-sided.

Fearnan had been one of Rob's gang and Nolan had sacked him without any explanation. Already, the Irishman was using his superior authority.

After Shaun went farther down the line to check on other work, Rob made a point of approaching the man named Kelly.

'What's this I hear about Fearnan? I didn't know he'd been given his cards.'

The man pretended to be surprised. 'Didn't the foreman tell you then? I thought you two were old friends!' Kelly gave a sly grin. 'I heard it was something to do with an incident that happened back at the Fort, Mr Stewart. Some girl was involved – a nurse from the infirmary.'

Rob drew in a breath. 'Go on, Kelly.'

The man shrugged. 'That's all I know about it, sir. Just that Fearnan and Mr Nolan were both there when it happened. Some of the men helped Fearnan pack his bag, but he couldn't say anything to them because Mr Nolan was there standing over him. They say the foreman saw Fearnan off on the train next morning. A bit strange, don't you think?'

The man was watching for his reaction, but Rob was too long in the tooth to be caught out by a gossip-monger.

'You can go back to work, Kelly. The break is over, and I don't want to hear any more of this gossip.'

Rob felt sick at heart.

There was one way he could find out the truth – he would tackle Beth. If some nurse from the infirmary was involved, then Beth was bound to have heard something.

Mhairi was sitting on the Stewarts' window-seat, knitting needles in her hands. Every-one in the household was insisting that she rested, but it did not come easily to someone who had led such a busy life. She looked down at the tiny garment which was quickly taking shape. The yarn was pale and creamy, its texture soft as swansdown. She pressed it against her cheek for a moment. In a drawer at home in Mallaig there were many such tiny garments like this one.

'Hello! And how's my favourite sister-in-law?' Beth picked up Mhairi's wrist and took her pulse. 'Better!' the nurse an-nounced with a confident smile. 'I told you, didn't I? Rest was all you needed.'

Beth had insisted that Mhairi sit with her feet up and now, flicking back a tartan rug, she examined the other girl's ankles for signs of swelling.

'Ah, that's more like it. Perhaps we might have a walk after lunch if you feel up to it?'

Mhairi's eyes shone. 'I should think so! I feel like an ornament sitting by this window all day!'

Later, they strolled down the hill together, Beth making sure they kept an easy pace. There was a seat above the sea-wall which looked down on the harbour, and from here they could see Catherine II sitting in dry-dock and her crew moving about its deck.

Fergus McCallum was there, too, his snow-white beard distinctive as he peered into the holds, then at the damaged hull. He appeared to linger where the name of the ship could just be distinguished on the seasoned timbers.

'Did you know Catherine was my grand-mother's name, and my mother's, too?' Mhairi revealed.

Beth's eyes widened. 'So that's how the name came about! There was a Catherine I, then?'

Mhairi nodded. 'Long before my time, Beth. My grandfather named her after his wife, and Father did likewise when Cath-erine I was lost at sea.'

She spoke in a matter-of-fact voice, but Beth could not help shivering. There was danger in every job, she supposed. When her father worked on the original building of the West Highland Line there had been several bad accidents.

Beth noted the set look on Mhairi's face. She stood up quickly.

'Right, that's it then. Enough exercise for one day. Let's go back to the house,' she suggested.

To her surprise, Mhairi put up no argument, and as they retraced their steps she drew in a sharp breath and steadied herself against the sea-wall.

'Mhairi, what's wrong?' Beth asked in concern.

'Just a stitch,' the other girl assured her.

They carried on uphill but at a much slower pace, and all the while Beth watched her sister-in-law with apprehension.

In the middle of the night, Beth awoke to find Will shaking her shoulder. She was immediately alert.

'It's Mhairi, isn't it?' Beth asked, pulling on her dressing-gown.

'She said I wasn't to disturb you, Beth, but I just had to come. It's too soon, isn't it? Mhairi's not due for another fortnight, but she's definitely having pains.'

Without waiting for more details, Beth

went into Will and Mhairi's bedroom. A quick examination of her sister-in-law told Beth all she needed to know. She looked at her watch, then spoke quietly to her brother.

'I think we should fetch Alec,' she told him. 'Here, I'll write down the address of his digs.'

Will stood looking at her in dismay. 'It's too soon, Beth. It's too soon!' he exclaimed, his voice breaking.

She took hold of his arm and led him outside. 'Perhaps so, Will, but your baby has decided otherwise. Now be a good lad and get Alec. You can use my bicycle. And, Will, go and waken Mother. I have a feeling I may need her help.'

As her brother went clattering downstairs, Beth couldn't help smiling. A few days ago he'd been facing a wild sea in a boat with a crippled engine, taking that terrible crisis in his stride. Yet now he didn't know where to turn.

Beth looked at her watch. There was enough time to dress properly and get on with a job she knew so well. At that moment she was grateful she had spent two years practising midwifery.

'What's going on?' a loud voice boomed.

Beth swung around to find Fergus McCallum at her elbow.

'Away back to your bed, Mr McCallum,' Beth advised, as she noted the alarm in his face. 'It's just your daughter having her baby.'

He stood there trembling.

'My wee Mhairi,' he kept saying, over and over.

When Beth looked at him, she saw tears trickling down his cheeks. She unexpectedly felt sorry for the old fisherman. 'Look, Mr McCallum,' she said, taking hold of his hands, 'everything will be just fine. I really know all about delivering babies. Now, if you're determined to stay up, why don't you go downstairs and get a fire going in the living-room? We could be in for a long night.'

The old man did as he was told.

Will came in, his face white, saying that Dr Buller was not at his digs and the local GP was also out on another urgent call.

'Don't they have midwives in Fort William?' Fergus demanded.

Will just shook his head before rushing upstairs with the bad news.

It seemed like an eternity before his son-in-law rejoined him in the living-room. Will looked bemused, and Fergus, jumping out of his chair, rushed across and shook him by the shoulders.

'What's wrong, lad?' he whispered, afraid for what he would hear. 'You must tell me the truth! I have to know!'

It was Janet Stewart, arriving with a tray in

116

her hands, who supplied the answer. 'Here, drink your tea, Fergus McCallum, and toast your lovely wee granddaughter!'

'I'll go up to Mhairi right now,' he decided. 'She'll want to see her father.'

'I'm sure she will, Fergus,' Janet replied, 'but not right now. Mhairi's very tired and needs sleep. Later, perhaps, after she's had some rest.'

He looked alarmed.

'But she's all right, isn't she? And the baby?'

'As right as any McCallum could be! Listen, won't you?' Janet opened the door a crack, and the faint sound of a baby crying filtered into the room.

Fergus's face split into a grin, then he settled contentedly into a chair.

Blissfully unaware, Rob Stewart was travelling back to Fort William on a service locomotive with the tunnel foreman. Shaun Nolan was to attend a meeting at the Company's office to discuss serious drilling difficulties on the Corpach cutting, whilst Rob, in answer to a message sent down the line from Janet earlier that morning, was on his way home.

They were forced to stand close together, but for the time being, all the past enmity Rob felt for his travelling companion had disappeared.

'Can you believe it?' he said, his elation

brimming over. 'I've got a granddaughter! Will's wife had her baby in the middle of the night.'

The Irishman knew all about the new arrival. He, himself, had delivered the note to Rob and arranged for his transport to the Fort.

'Congratulations,' he offered quietly. Then he added, 'Both well, I trust?'

The older man beamed. 'That's what Janet says, here in her note!' He took it from his pocket and read it for the umpteenth time, then turned to his companion.

'The baby arrived two weeks early, you see, and it was my own daughter who delivered the child. You'll remember Beth, when you lived with us? She's a nurse now, at the infirmary,' Rob went on with pride. 'As a matter of fact, Beth is to take charge of nursing once the site hospital opens at Lochailort.'

The Irishman didn't reveal that he knew about Beth Stewart's posting, too. After all, he'd driven the auburn-haired girl to the site himself, along with that long-faced doctor who had looked at him so jealously whenever he attempted to put a word in.

He sighed.

It was some time now since Rosa had died, but he would have given the earth to be going home to his wife and their baby daughter.

He gave himself a mental shake. A foreman had to be on hand at all times at a camp while work was in progress, and for the foreseeable future, he would be spending most of his time at Lochailort. Hopefully, he'd be kept too busy to think of what might have been with the wife he'd adored.

Shaun Nolan's Request

It was later in the morning before Rob managed to corner Beth in the garden. His daughter, with wooden clothes-pegs clamped between her teeth, was standing on tiptoe to hang out nappies on the line.

'She's a great wee thing, isn't she?' he remarked to Beth.

She nodded dumbly before removing the last two pins from her mouth and attaching a linen square to the line. 'She's all that, and she has a fine pair of lungs into the bargain. Would you listen to her?'

Although the bedroom window was only open a few inches, they could hear the baby crying.

'Hungry again,' Beth explained cheerfully. 'Did you come out to the garden for anything special?' she inquired as she picked up the empty laundry-basket.

Rob clapped a hand over his mouth. 'I forgot – your mother sent me to pull leeks and carrots for soup!'

His daughter laughed. 'Here, let me help you,' she offered.

They worked together companionably. With winter's approach, the ground was hard and unwieldy, and Rob was red-faced with exertion as he dug up the vegetables.

He brushed the earth off his hands, and paused to look at his daughter.

'Here, lass, before we go back into the house, could you clear up a matter that was brought to my attention at work yesterday? It's about an incident that took place down by the viaduct. Did you hear anything about it at the hospital?'

Beth felt her heart-beat quicken, and her hands tightened on the laundry-basket. 'Where did you say you heard this, Father?' she asked, trying to give herself time.

'A man on the site at Corpach was going on about it. One of the tunnel labourers, a fellow called Fearnan, was involved. Shaun Nolan sacked him and packed him off on a train next morning.

'Apparently some nurse from the infirmary was involved,' he explained. 'If you know anything about it, Beth, I'd be obliged if you'd tell me. Fearnan's mates feel he was unfairly dismissed.'

The basket fell from Beth's numbed hands.

'Unfairly dismissed? He was lucky not to have been arrested!' she blurted out before she could stop herself.

'So you *do* know something,' Rob declared. 'What was this about a nurse–' He broke off as he realised how distressed his daughter was. 'Oh, lass, not you! It wasn't you?' He pulled his daughter into his arms. 'Please, you must tell me exactly what happened.'

Beth sighed. Just when she thought she could forget about that incident, here it was back to haunt her.

As she began to recount the sorry tale, Rob Stewart's face grew grey. 'And you didn't say one word. You came home and said nothing?'

'I couldn't bring myself to,' she admitted. 'When Shaun brought me home that night, I could hear you all talking and laughing in the front room. Will had just returned home, remember, and everyone sounded so happy. How could I spoil things?'

Rob hugged her close. 'After all the things I've said about Nolan, if it hadn't been for him...' He paused. 'Beth, I can understand why you tried to play it down, for our sakes, but why didn't Nolan report the matter to the police?'

Beth laid an urgent hand on his arm.

'Because I asked him not to, Father,' she said quietly. 'Shaun wanted to call in the constabulary, but I decided against that, so long as he promised to have the man sent away.' Now it was her turn to console. 'Look, Father, there was no real harm done,' she assured him. 'It's all in the past and best forgotten.'

As they walked slowly back to the house, she took his hand in hers.

'Promise you won't say anything to the family? I'd rather we kept this to ourselves.'

'Say nothing?' he repeated. 'Not even to your mother?'

'Especially not to Mother!' Beth insisted. 'Don't you see, Father, she would never have a moment's peace, worrying whenever I was out.'

Reluctantly he gave in. 'If that's what you really want, Beth, so be it.'

It was well into the afternoon before Alec Buller arrived at the Stewarts' cottage. Beth met him at the door.

'Sorry, Beth,' he began to apologise, 'it's been frantic down at the infirmary. I've been in Theatre all morning. This is the first chance I've had to get away.'

Beth frowned. 'But where were you last night, Alec? I sent Will to fetch you, and you weren't at your digs.'

The young surgeon spread his hands. 'At

the hotel where the railway contractors are staying, would you believe? I was summoned to appear at a special meeting,' he explained. 'I'm afraid we sat up half the night talking and discussing plans–'

'Plans?' Beth interrupted. 'What plans?'

Alec looked at her in astonishment. 'Why, plans for our move to the site hospital! Have you forgotten so fast?' he asked in exasperation.

Beth was puzzled. 'But that's months away, surely?'

He shook his head rather impatiently. 'No, Beth, that's what I thought, too, but they want us to make a start one week from now. I know it's short notice and the workmen are still busy, but Mr McAlpine feels at least one of us should be present for security reasons.'

'One of us?' Beth repeated uncertainly, realising that Alec seemed uncomfortable.

'Yes, I'm afraid so, and it looks as though it will have to be you, Beth.'

She gasped.

'You see,' Alec explained, 'they have still to arrange my replacement at the infirmary and–'

'–and I suppose, with Sister Baxter back, I'm surplus to requirements at the moment,' she put in. 'You mean I'm going to be up at Lochailort on my own?'

Alec's face was full of embarrassment. 'Well, not quite, Beth. Another nurse is due to arrive, too, and I'll be joining you just as soon as I'm replaced,' he pointed out.

'It's all happening so soon, Alec,' the girl protested. 'I'd hoped to be around for Mhairi for a while.'

'Ah, yes, Mhairi's baby.' Alec seemed relieved to change the subject. 'I'm truly sorry I was unavailable when Will called at my digs. I did leave a note on the hallstand for my landlady, but she tells me she didn't see it until this morning. I suppose you had to call in the GP?'

'He was out on a call, too,' Beth explained, 'and the baby came so fast, Mother and I had to do what was necessary.'

His eyes widened, then he signalled for her to follow him upstairs.

'They're both doing remarkably well,' he admitted, after he'd examined Mhairi and the baby. 'I could kick myself for not being around, Beth. I think we should keep an eye on them both for the next few days. I'll make a note for the local midwife to make regular calls, but I must say the McCallums seem a resilient lot.'

'And the Stewarts,' she reminded him promptly.

Alec smiled. 'Ah, yes, the Stewarts. Who could forget them?'

Later, they walked in the garden together, discussing the imminent move to Loch-ailort.

When they came to the gate, he turned to make sure they were unobserved from the house, then, reaching out, drew her towards him.

Beth raised her face eagerly towards his.

'Oh, Beth!' Alec's face was filled with longing. 'I've missed you so and I don't mean in Theatre.'

When Alec lowered his head towards her, Beth's lips met his without hesitation.

Beth had been installed in the camp hospital for two days where she discovered a team of painters working in the main ward.

'Do you think,' she demanded edgily, 'you could leave that window open?' A soothing shade of green, the pamphlet had described it, but Beth was unconvinced. The ward walls looked a rather sickly shade, and the smell of turpentine and paint pervaded everything.

Boxes of files had arrived earlier that morning. Beth was busy transporting these from the main entrance hall and arranging them in a little office beside the ward.

Saying goodbye to the infirmary staff had been a wrench. Beth had not realised how much she was going to miss them, but when it came to the parting with her family, one would have thought she was emigrating to the Americas.

Everyone was weeping, particularly Mhairi,

who had only cheered up when Beth told her she would be home for Christmas and the christening, too, when she was to be the baby's godmother.

Now she was on her own in this rather makeshift place they insisted upon calling a hospital. Would it really be able to cope with emergencies, she asked herself?

With the furniture inside, it looked small, and the kitchen facilities they'd been promised had still to arrive.

Thankfully, there was a canteen on the site, and she survived on fresh bread and the odd hot dish sent up by the cook.

Today, the other nurse was due to arrive, and Beth had tried to make their living quarters more attractive, gathering wild grasses on the hillside and a few roses surviving in the schoolhouse garden.

She hoped they would get along together. Another woman could prove comforting in such a male-dominated site.

The sound of cartwheels brought her scurrying outside. She was just in time to see a tall girl being helped down from the passenger seat of a wagon by none other than the tunnel foreman, Shaun Nolan.

'This is Nurse O'Malley,' Shaun informed Beth as the freckle-faced woman came striding towards her. 'You'll be all right with this one, Sister Stewart. She hails from my own part of the world.'

'Away with you, man.' The nurse gave the foreman an indulgent smile. 'I can prove myself, thank you, without your fine recommendations.'

Beth held out her hand, and felt relieved to discover that the nurse they had sent to her was an open sort of person and not in the least shy.

'It was a rare laugh, Sister,' Nurse O'Malley said as she cheerfully accepted a cup of tea. 'You see, I come from the next village, and when Shaun's mother heard that I was travelling to work over here, nothing would do but I take a parcel of food for her boy.'

Shaun was opening the tightly-wrapped parcel as Bridget spoke.

He smiled as he held up a batch of soda bread for their inspection, but Beth noticed that he slipped into his pocket a thick envelope, hidden inside the parcel.

As he did not seem in any hurry to be going, Beth poured him a cup of tea, too.

'What's the awful smell?' he inquired.

Beth pointed to the newly-painted walls.

'Won't that cause your poor patients to have a relapse?'

'It's supposed to be restful!' she retorted defensively. 'Now, if you'll excuse us, Shaun, I must show Bridget where she'll be sleeping.'

The Irishman politely stood up as the two

women left. Once alone, he quickly drew the envelope from his pocket and read the letter from his mother. His face seemed to grow older and his shoulders drooped.

'Oh, dear Lord,' he murmured to himself, 'this is what I dreaded most. What on earth am I going to do now?'

As he heard the two women coming back downstairs, he seemed determined not to display his emotions and, returning the envelope to his pocket, straightened himself.

'Thanks for the tea, Sister Stewart, I'll be seeing you both soon. From now on, I'll be living down at the camp, so if you have any worries at all, just send for me. Remember what I told you the first time you visited here? Just pull on that bell out there, if you want help in a hurry.' He waved and climbed back aboard the wagon.

'A nice lad, Shaun Nolan,' Bridget said conversationally, as she and Beth went inside again. 'What a shame he's had all that tragedy.'

'Tragedy, Bridget?'

The new nurse looked up somewhat surprised. 'Why, yes, Sister. You know, that poor wife of his, dying the way she did? Sure, it was the talk of the village.'

'Then you know Shaun Nolan well?' Beth queried.

'Not all that well, Sister, but we come from neighbouring villages and we're both from farming stock. I used to see him at local dances, but that was before he took himself off to see the world.'

The nurse crossed the room to stare out of the window. 'Isn't this a fine place? Would you look at those great fellows over there...' She was pointing to the mountains which surrounded them and Beth got the distinct impression Bridget was attempting to change the subject.

Beth waited impatiently. 'You were saying about Mr Nolan?' she prompted.

Bridget looked uncomfortable. 'Well, if you must know, Sister, it was awfully sad – Shaun lost his wife in childbirth. He married a Spanish girl, you see. We all thought it a bit strange when he sent his new wife home to stay with his parents, although he went on working abroad, but it was his business, after all.'

Beth poured out two cups of tea and handed one to Bridget.

'I only saw Rosa a couple of times. She was beautiful,' the Irish girl went on dreamily. 'Black hair, she had, black as coal, and a complexion like porcelain. I've never seen such pure skin colour. Now, I don't know about you, Sister, but that's not a good sign where I come from. In addition, she didn't adapt well to our damp climate.'

'And you say that she died in childbirth?'

Bridget looked at Beth pleadingly. 'I

shouldn't be telling you this at all, Sister. You see, Shaun refuses to talk about Rosa,' she explained. 'I tried to bring up the subject when we were driving here, and he just about bit my nose off. Of course, there are some who say he blames himself for her death and – oh dear!'

She stopped talking and stared at Beth. 'You won't tell him I've been discussing Rosa?' she begged. 'He'd never forgive me for talking about her to strangers.'

It seemed obvious that the Irish girl regretted her candour, but her last remark stung Beth.

'He's not exactly a stranger to me, Bridget,' she said a little frostily. 'You see, when he worked on the first line, to Fort William, Shaun Nolan used to board at our house.'

For a moment the girl opposite seemed taken aback.

'I didn't know that, Sister. Shaun never mentioned that. Still, if he's so friendly with you, then I suppose he'll tell you about his troubles, all in good time.'

During the next few days Beth was to discover that in Bridget O'Malley she'd found an invaluable assistant and cheerful companion.

The Irish girl proved an energetic worker, and with her able assistance the site hospital was quickly taking shape.

Soon after her arrival at Lochailort, Bridget stood watching the painting squad still working in the ward. 'Those fellows are taking their time, are they not?'

Beth shook her head in frustration.

'I agree, but there's nothing much we can do about it. I suppose they know their business.'

'Is that so?' Bridget replied sharply. Then she winked at Beth.

'Watch this.' She marched across to the charge-hand and pointed to the window-frames to which the men were putting finishing touches with slow, laborious strokes.

'Tell me now, are you lot trained painters or are you just practising?' she demanded.

The men were quite taken aback, but as Bridget continued to watch, they put on a real spurt, and by the end of the day their job was completed.

The two women watched as they packed their equipment into a barrow and prepared to leave.

Bridget stood at the front door to see them off.

'Ay,' one man remarked, 'you'd make a rare gaffer in any trade!'

Bridget grinned at Beth. 'That's the way to deal with malingerers, Sister!'

'I'm sure you're right,' Beth agreed. 'Now

perhaps we can get on with our proper jobs.'

Already men were arriving at the Lochailort site hospital with various medical complaints.

Shaun, too, became a fairly regular visitor. He would bring along tunnel labourers to the outpatients' surgery at regular intervals.

On his third visit, he cornered Beth in the office.

'When's your doctor due to arrive?' he asked bluntly.

Beth shrugged. 'Your guess is as good as mine,' she replied. 'Why do you ask? Are you finding our nursing abilities inadequate?'

Shaun flushed. 'Of course I don't. You two are doing excellent work here,' he assured her. 'I just have something I'd like to discuss with him.'

'Can't I help? I'm fairly well qualified, you know.'

He looked at her doubtfully. 'I … I'm anxious about a friend of mine. You see…'

'Go on, Shaun,' Beth prompted gently. 'Anything you tell me will be treated in the strictest confidence.'

He still looked uncomfortable. 'It's rather personal and I'd prefer not to talk about it here. I wonder if…' He hesitated again. 'Look, when do you come off duty?'

She told him and he pursed his lips thoughtfully.

132

'We could walk down by the loch, I suppose, but there are always workmen milling about down there, too. No, I've got a better idea,' Shaun decided, brightening a little. 'When I have time off, I have the use of a dinghy. Sometimes I do a bit of night fishing – I find it relaxing. Would you join me?'

Beth knew that he was looking for her advice as a friend rather than as a nurse, and smiled. 'I love fishing,' she assured him. 'Father used to take me out with him...' She stopped suddenly.

Shaun was watching her closely.

'Of course, he took you, too, didn't he, when you boarded with us?' she remembered.

Shaun nodded. 'Rob taught me to cast my first fly. Those were good days.'

A shadow seemed to flit across his lean face for a moment before he spoke again. 'You'll come, then?'

'I've never been known to refuse an invitation to go fishing!' Beth promised.

The Touch Of His Lips

Janet Stewart reached deep into the salt drawer and scooped out a ladleful. On Mondays she always made broth, and the mutton cooking on the range was just about ready. The stock would provide a fine base for her soup.

Beth had only been gone a few weeks, but already her mother sorely missed her. There had always been a warm bond between them.

When Beth worked at the infirmary, her hours of duty had seemed awkward, but they still saw a lot of each other. Now, installed in the isolated site hospital at Lochailort, Beth was forced to live in. With only an occasional mail coach or steamer, Janet realised that until the railway extension reached the area, Beth's visits home would prove difficult, if not impossible.

Still, there were compensations. She had Will and Mhairi staying with her until the baby was strong enough to travel. Janet smiled whenever she thought of her first granddaughter, who had rapidly become the centre of attraction in the Stewart household.

She looked around her kitchen suspiciously. Surely she could smell tobacco?

Fergus McCallum sat in the ingle-nook, and as Janet stared across she was just in time to see him put his pipe into his jacket pocket.

On the point of tackling him about smoking in the kitchen, Janet had second thoughts. She'd grown used to the tall old man in her kitchen. He seemed to enjoy its warmth and the smell of her cooking. Besides, with Rob working regularly at Corpach these days, she had to admit Fergus was always ready to do the odd chore for her.

When would he be going back to Mallaig, she wondered. It seemed this would-be tyrant was in no hurry to go home, and seemed content to play the doting grandfather. To everyone's surprise, Mhairi's tiny daughter had stolen Fergus's heart, too. Once, when he was holding the baby for a moment whilst her bath was being filled, Janet had watched the old man's eyes fill with tears. But if Fergus was softening so far as the new arrival was concerned, he had not lost any of his hard-headed business sense.

As they'd sat down to breakfast earlier that morning, he'd turned towards his son-in-law and dropped a bombshell.

'I've decided to let Catherine II go,' he

announced. 'The Salvage Inspector tells me it would cost far too much to make her seaworthy.'

Janet watched Will's face as the old man spoke. It looked as though her son had been dealt a physical blow, but it was Mhairi who sprang immediately to her husband's side.

'How could you, Father, and at a time like this?' she accused. 'What can Will do now, when he doesn't have a boat? He's been working all the hours God sends to get that engine right.'

For a moment Fergus's face showed its old stubbornness. 'And what do you know about it?' he retorted. 'I wish, Mhairi, that you would leave men's work to the men.' Then he turned to Will and spoke sharply. 'Since you've nothing better to do this morning, young man, you might walk with me down to the jetty where we can discuss this matter properly–' He glanced across at his daughter and added '–without inter-ruption.'

Will nodded. 'If you wish, Mr McCallum, I'll just go to get my oilskins.'

Mhairi quickly followed her husband upstairs. Janet could hear their hushed voices, and her heart went out to them.

Their future must seem bleak with a new baby to add to their worries.

Fergus and Will left shortly afterwards, and Mhairi wandered into the kitchen. She

136

looked unhappy and worked by her mother-in-law's side without speaking.

'I know Catherine II wasn't a great boat,' Mhairi said at last, 'but it was ours, and Will worked so hard on her. I just can't understand Father's attitude. Before, he would hear nothing said against Catherine II. Now, he's scrapping her, just like that.'

When the two men had still not returned after a couple of hours, Janet could see that Mhairi was growing anxious.

'Look, lass, feed your bairn and put her down for a nap,' Janet suggested. 'Then you and I will have a nice cup of tea.'

The words were hardly out of Janet's mouth when the sound of footsteps on the path could be heard. The door burst open and Will came rushing in. He strode across the room, caught his wife in his arms and began to waltz her round the kitchen.

'You'll never guess what your father has done, Mhairi!' he exclaimed. 'Just bought us a new boat from Findlay's boatyard! A real beauty, too, and do you know what we're going to call her?'

Mhairi shook her head, her eyes moving to the tall figure of Fergus, bending his head in order to enter the low doorway into Janet's kitchen.

'Catherine III! We're going to name her after our little girl. Now, what do you think about that?'

137

The pride in Will's voice made a lump come to his mother's throat. She gazed at Fergus as he took his favourite seat in the corner. Her expression softened. Despite everything she'd heard about this cantankerous old man in the past, it seemed he had a tender heart after all.

A moment later, the old man lived up to his reputation.

'Ay, and I hope you'll bring in a better catch from now on,' he warned, pointing at Will. 'You won't have to waste time repairing an engine. Catherine III has to pay her way – do you hear?'

As Beth left the hospital at Lochailort, she felt a sense of relief. Since Shaun's invitation to go fishing, she'd felt embarrassed about telling Bridget O'Malley. In the end, the Irish girl seemed intrigued, but said little.

Shaun was waiting for her beside a small jetty. She'd taken time to dress warmly and now pulled her thick, woollen cloak closer.

He nodded his approval. 'It can get very cold out on the water after the sun goes down.'

Beth had begun to doubt her wisdom in answering Shaun's plea for help. She could just imagine what Alec Buller would have to say about such impulsive behaviour. Beth raised her chin defiantly. But then, Alec was

138

not here, she reminded herself. Instead, he had left her to look after the hospital whilst he stayed on in town.

She hadn't forgiven Alec for his prolonged absence, nor for the fact that he hadn't attempted to get in touch since her arrival at Lochailort. After all, it was easy enough to send a letter down the line. Her father did so regularly, giving her news about home.

A breeze from the loch made Beth shiver as Shaun helped her climb down the narrow, rickety steps attached to the end of the jetty, then aboard the dinghy. He looked at her anxiously, then, making sure she was comfortably seated, tucked a rug about her knees.

Silently, she watched as he took his own seat and gathered in the oars.

Tonight, the loch was still and mirror-like. Beth felt it would mist over if she so much as breathed on it. High behind them, mountains rose silhouetted against the sky, the tallest of these already tipped by snow. She watched Shaun's easy, rhythmic strokes, the blades of the oars dipping through the water, then studied his face. He looked typically Irish, she decided, his hair dark and with eyes that always seemed to have a faraway look in them.

When they reached the centre of the loch, Shaun pulled two fishing-rods from the bottom of the boat. He handed one to her, and she looked carefully at Shaun's collection of flies. They were obviously handmade and showed great attention to detail. She took pleasure in making her selection.

'Another craft your father taught me,' he said softly and Beth looked up. 'I haven't forgotten all his kindness, you know, even if what's happened recently makes you think otherwise.'

When she didn't reply he went on.

'I did a lot of soul-searching, Beth, before I took that foreman's job.'

'Why did you?' she asked quickly, and as he looked her straight in the eyes, she noticed how his lips tightened.

'I knew, on this occasion, that I was the better man for the job. Before you accuse me of big-headedness, let me explain. In ordinary circumstances, there's no-one I'd rather have in charge of a tunnel than your father, but the rock we're dealing with here is another matter,' he said seriously. 'I've worked with material like it in Canada and learnt the hard way about its dangers, and what to look out for.'

'I'm not as ignorant as you think, Shaun,' Beth broke in. 'After all, I'm a tunneller's daughter, and I know about that hard rock and how all your drills are breaking...'

Shaun's eyes widened in surprise. 'Well, that's part of it, for sure,' he admitted, 'although Mr McAlpine may have come up

140

with the answer to that problem already. Yes, it's true,' he assured her. 'He watched his dentist use a foot pump when drilling his teeth. It was powered by water.'

'What difference did that make?' Beth demanded.

Shaun grinned at her. 'He's just given the civil engineer the go-ahead to develop the idea on a big scale. Can you imagine it, Beth, a water turbine to power our drills? It will mean creating a dam, of course.'

Beth gasped. 'And all that came from a visit to a dentist?' she asked doubtfully.

Shaun sat upright and cast a line far out over the loch. 'You know what they say, Beth, from little acorns...' He watched as Beth flicked her own rod back then made an expert cast, her fly landing far away.

The pair grew silent as they began to fish in earnest.

Lights were beginning to flicker from the camp huts on the other side of the loch, and Beth could hear the sound of voices from the shore.

'Shaun,' she prompted a little hesitantly, 'you didn't bring me here just to fish, remember? There's something you wanted to discuss.'

The rod tightened in his hand, but he didn't look at her. 'It's a medical matter, Beth. It's about a friend of mine back home,' he explained. 'There's a baby, and it seems she's not too well at the moment...'

Beth remained silent for a moment, then nodded in the growing dusk.

'Babies are often sick, Shaun. Sometimes it's just the feeding,' she pointed out.

'Not that sort of sickness,' he broke in, his voice tense. 'I mean really sick, not able to breathe properly and–'

'It would help if you could explain the symptoms, Shaun,' she urged.

He began to repeat them word for word, as though he had learned them by rote, while Beth listened attentively.

'This friend of mine lives away from home, you understand, and his mother cares for the child,' he explained. 'She's really worried because sometimes the baby can't seem to get a breath, and coughs and wheezes half the night.'

His voice broke, and Beth wished she could take his hand to comfort him.

'What does the doctor think?' she asked quietly.

He turned towards her, his expression despairing. 'He dismisses it as just a minor childish setback...'

'I wonder if it's whooping-cough,' Beth said. 'The symptoms you've described remind me of when there was an epidemic in the Fort. Are there any other cases in the area?'

'I'm not sure, and you see, the doctor's in a town a long way from the village, so he wouldn't know either. But you mean it could be something as simple as that?'

'There's nothing simple about whooping-cough, Shaun, but with care, most children get over it,' Beth assured him. 'I've nursed a few cases in my day.'

His eyes gleamed with new hope.

'Don't take my word for it,' she insisted. 'I'm not in the habit of making a long-distance diagnosis. Your friend's mother should ask for another opinion. Tell her to take the child to the local hospital to have a thorough check-up.'

'Oh, I will. I certainly will. I'll write a letter straightaway.'

Both feeling lighter-hearted, they turned their attention to fishing once more. Beth cast in the direction where, earlier, she'd noticed a small plop. Almost immediately she felt a tug on the line and began to reel in.

'It's a big one!' she gasped, feeling the sheer strength of the pull.

Quickly, Shaun left his seat and came to help. When the fish leapt out of the water, they saw it was a salmon, and it put up a brave fight.

'You've got him!' Shaun cried at last. 'Oh, would you look at that beauty!' Together they brought the shimmering fish aboard.

Beth looked down to the bottom of the boat where the salmon lay, still wriggling within the landing-net. She could see its sleek shape and beautiful, silvery skin. She came to a sudden decision. 'Let it go, please, Shaun.'

He looked at her in disbelief. 'I don't understand,' he protested. 'You both fought a fair fight and you won. I thought you said you liked to go fishing!'

'I do, but I can't bring myself to kill such a lovely thing.'

Shaking his head, he did as she asked and they watched as the beautiful creature swam away with a flick of its tail.

There was a long silence between them, then Shaun said quietly. 'You're a strange one, Beth. I've thrown back the odd fish myself, but only tiddlers – not a beauty like that.'

The moon had appeared above the trees, and stars were beginning to twinkle overhead.

'Shall we go back?' he asked her.

She looked embarrassed.

'I've spoiled your evening, haven't I?'

'On the contrary, I've found it most illuminating.'

'But you came out to fish, Shaun....'

'In more ways than you imagine, Beth. I think we'll call it a night. Anyway, I've got a

144

letter to write.' He rowed them to the shore, but this time Beth imagined there was renewed strength in his strokes, and his eyes looked bright and optimistic. Only one thing saddened her. Why couldn't he trust her with the whole truth – that it was his own child he'd been referring to out there on the loch...

Lights shone from the hospital windows as they made their way up the track. Beth could see an oil lamp flickering in the window of the staff sitting-room, and wondered why Bridget had stayed up so late. The Irish nurse had told Beth that she was going to read in bed.

'Well, I'll say good-night, Beth, and thanks for your advice.'

She turned with a smile, for despite the episode with the salmon, she'd enjoyed her evening on the loch and, indeed, the company of this surprising man. She wasn't prepared for what happened next.

His two hands gently enfolded her face, and she sensed more than felt the butterfly touch of his lips on hers. 'Bless you, dear girl, for the hope you've given me,' he whispered.

'Shaun, I only...' she began.

But he was gone, striding down the path.

Straightening her shoulders, Beth walked inside, making her way along the corridor to the staff sitting-room.

There, by the fire, sat Bridget, wrapped in

a blue dressing-gown, sipping a large mug of cocoa, and opposite, in a matching armchair was Alec Buller.

'Alec!' Beth exclaimed. 'When on earth did you arrive? There's no ferry at this hour.'

He stood up slowly, and she noticed that his expression seemed stiff. He turned and thanked Bridget for the hot drink.

The Irish girl rose and, giving Beth a searching look, made her way upstairs.

When she had gone, Alec turned to Beth once more.

'I got a lift from a fishing-boat, then managed to get a ride from a man at the jetty up here. I've been looking forward all day to seeing you again, Beth, and I hoped you'd been missing me. It seems, however, that you've been too busy enjoying yourself with Nolan for that!'

Eyes wide with disbelief, Beth stood and listened to Alec Buller's reprimand.

'I thought I could expect better from you, Beth. After all, I did leave you in charge here during my absence, yet you didn't feel it was out of place to leave a new assistant alone in this isolated hospital, while you and Nolan–'

Beth's expression of surprise was quickly being replaced by resentment. When, at last, she found her voice, it sounded icy. 'He asked for help, if you must know. I thought that answering calls for help was part of our job!'

Alec Buller was unimpressed. 'Help, you say? So you decided the best way to fit in this good deed was to go fishing?' He sneered.

Beth shook her head angrily. 'Shaun decided it would be easier to confide his problem where we could not be disturbed. Anyway, I don't know why I'm defending myself. I take it I'm entitled to some free time, or should I consider myself a prisoner here for twenty-four hours a day?' she retorted.

For a moment he seemed taken aback by her spirited retaliation.

'Certainly not,' Alec said hastily. 'Once we get a proper rota system organised, there will be plenty of free time for all of us.'

'There was no surgery,' she reminded him coldly, 'and there were no in-patients, as you would have gathered had you found time to glance in the ward... Sir!'

This last title seemed to have a demoralising effect upon the hospital's new resident doctor. Alec's lean face froze. 'Beth, please,' he began, but she turned on her heel.

'Now, if you don't mind, I'll go to see that your room is ready. We would have arranged for a fire to be lit and your bed made up had we known you were arriving tonight,' she snapped over her shoulder.

Alec's face was a study in bewilderment as he watched Beth adopt her professional role. He had often watched her treat difficult patients in this manner, but never dreamed that he would be on the receiving end.

Now, he decided, was not the appropriate time to say he'd intended to surprise her with his unexpected arrival!

Without another word, he collected his luggage and followed her upstairs.

The next few weeks were to prove busy ones for the hospital staff at Lochailort. With the arrival of supplies by sea, there was an air of activity everywhere, and not a day seemed to pass without some minor mishap, with at least one workman being admitted to the out-patients department.

Beth recalled how her father had explained the plans for an imaginative piece of civil engineering at Glenfinnan. Now, at long last Glenfinnan Viaduct, with its proposed twenty-one arches, was underway.

It was common knowledge that rival builders were making scathing remarks about the contractor's revolutionary ideas, particularly his use of mass concrete.

Beth, having had the pleasure of meeting Concrete Bob in person and having heard him talk, refused to listen to their derogatory comments. To her, Robert McAlpine was a genius who inspired confidence.

While she was working beside Alec in the

surgery one morning, a letter arrived from the contractor himself. As he read it, the doctor pursed his lips.

'Oh, no! It's an invitation to join the governors to observe their first tunnel explosion.'

Beth did not miss the note of dismay in his voice.

'I'm not really into firework displays,' he admitted. 'I think we'll give it a miss, don't you?'

She couldn't help feeling disappointed, but decided not to let this show. Instead, she glanced at the letter after Alec laid it down on the table.

'Did you read the last paragraph?' she queried.

'Oh, I see what you mean. Some trouble with drills, and they'd appreciate medical staff on hand, just in case of an accident. I suppose this puts a different complexion on the matter.'

Then the arrival of an injured workman took up the attention of both doctor and nurse.

After examining the new patient, Alec turned to Beth.

'This head wound won't need to be stitched, Sister, but perhaps you'd put a dressing on it,' he said in his most professional manner.

'Certainly, Doctor,' Beth responded, and

turned to the tall workman sitting on a chair in the middle of the surgery. He was a big man, well over six feet, with a shock of reddish hair.

Beth felt that there was something familiar about his features, yet she was certain he had never been treated before.

'How did you manage to do this, then?' she asked, examining the wound on the crown of his head.

The tall workman seemed embarrassed.

'I forgot to duck, Sister,' he confessed. 'Sure, they don't make doorways over here for lads of my height.'

'Well, it's not too bad, as the doctor said, but I'll have to cut away some of your hair so I can put on a dressing, Mr...?' She glanced down at the card which he had brought with him. 'Mr O'Malley?' she asked, putting two and two together. 'Not Bryan O'Malley, by any chance?'

He winced as she dabbed the wound with antiseptic.

'The very same, ma'am, but will you go easy with that stuff? It stings like mad.'

Very carefully she trimmed the hair around the wound, then applied a dressing.

The man stood up and glanced ruefully at his reflection in a mirror.

'I won't stand much chance with the girls now,' he said. 'Not that there are many sweet ladies around these parts – begging your pardon – with the exception of your good self, of course.'

'Oh, I don't know about that,' Beth replied with a smile. 'There's a girl through in Reception who'll be glad to spare you a few words when you hand in your card.'

He touched his forehead and smiled before moving into the next room.

Beth heard a delighted cry.

'It's yourself, Bridget!'

'Bryan!' the Irish nurse exclaimed. 'I might have known you'd find your way up here sooner or later. What have you been doing this time?'

Beth closed the door quietly on Bridget's reunion with her brother.

'Three Men Are Trapped...'

Rob Stewart had been busy rock cutting outside Corpach for the past two months. Track laying had come to an abrupt halt when the navvies reached a high escarpment blocking their path.

This was the sort of work he'd been used to in the old days, and he felt that he was coming into his own at last. The engineers were ready to blast their way through.

It had taken days of planning, and there

had been arguments between Shaun Nolan and himself as to which type of explosives should be used, but at last everything was ready. When he was given the signal from the foreman, bugles were to be sounded giving warning of the forthcoming blast.

On a hillside separated by a valley from the workings, a marquee had been assembled. Outside it was gathered a group of invited guests, directors of the railway company and local landowners through whose estates the line would eventually run.

Rob gazed up the scree slope. Those fine fellows were making sure they would not be in any danger, he thought, but at the same time had placed chairs at strategic positions along the ridge in order to have an unrestricted view of the proceedings.

Shaun Nolan had been going back and forward between the workmen and the official party. Earlier, he'd stopped to give Rob final instructions.

'I suppose we'd better provide them with their bit of entertainment, Rob. Once they go off to the hotel then we can get on with the real work, eh?'

His assistant nodded, looking up at the young foreman on the horse the company had provided. Shaun seemed completely at ease in the saddle. Rob was about to remark upon this when Shaun forestalled him.

'We always used outriders to warn of

explosions in Canada, Rob. They're faster than trying to get about by cart. Now, I'll go up and say that we're about ready...'

Over the last few weeks Rob's respect for the foreman had grown. Shaun inspired confidence, was positive when he gave orders, but listened to any reasonable complaint from the men.

Indeed, it had been in Rob's mind to ask Shaun to join the family at Fort William this Christmas to be part of the festivities and to be present when his first granddaughter was christened. He would never forget how Shaun had come to Beth's rescue when she'd been frightened by one of the workmen, even if the Irishman preferred to play that deed down.

Rob stared through his field-glasses at the people on the hill, and for the first time noticed two women dressed in nurse's uniform.

On the hillside, Beth turned to stare at the assembled guests. The directors wore thick overcoats and top hats, whilst landowners had settled for more comfortable tweeds.

One man, who wore a monocle, looked very bored indeed. Beth heard him say to Robert McAlpine, 'You might have picked a better day for your fireworks, Robert. It's pretty bleak up here.'

Certainly the weather was turning colder by the hour. Frost hung in the air, and Beth drew her cloak closer around her shoulders.

The monocled man stamped his feet.

'Yes,' Concrete Bob agreed dryly, 'but if you want us to complete the job in the time allotted, then we have to make use of every day the good lord sends. We must take precautions, sir, with the hard rock down there, and cannot afford to grow careless. Pray be patient. You'll have your action soon enough.'

Beth had noticed Shaun Nolan the moment she arrived at the site. He was not easy to miss mounted on his big, grey horse.

It was a pity he seemed so busy, she reflected. There would be no time today to speak to him about his sick child in Ireland. Beth felt certain Shaun had noticed their small group when they arrived in the makeshift ambulance, yet he gave no sign.

When Robert McAlpine gave final instructions, Shaun remounted his horse. Once in the saddle, he turned in Beth's direction and, removing his wide hat, nodded to her before sending his horse forward to pick its way down the scree slope to the cutting. She could feel her cheeks burning and, when she returned, became aware that Alec Buller was watching her closely.

The next moment bugles sounded, giving warning of the forthcoming explosion. The onlookers waited nervously and, as the seconds ticked away, a silence hung over the waiting crowd. There was a muffled boom and Beth felt the earth shake under her feet. Her heart missed a beat as she realised her father was still down in the cutting where the explosion had taken place.

There were sounds of cheering from the valley below, as workmen threw their hats in the air and clapped.

When it was declared safe, the dignitaries crept forward to gaze once more through field-glasses. Where once a tall cliff had been, now there was a gaping hole and a sea of boulders ready to be shifted by hundreds of willing hands, once the cloud of dust settled.

Mr McAlpine turned to his guests. 'A good job, gentlemen, wouldn't you agree? Now, let's retire to the refreshment tent for lunch,' he proposed. He came across to where Alec and the hospital party stood. 'You'll join us, won't you?' he invited. 'Now they've shown a white flag down there, I'm thankful to say there will be no call on your professional services today.'

The dust was settling at last, and Rob Stewart, about to send his men in to start the clearing up, heard the sound of footsteps. Shaun Nolan had tethered his horse to a tree far enough from the danger area, and he hurried across.

'A moment, Rob, if you please.' He bent down to examine the rocks strewn around the entrance. 'Just as I thought...' He stood up and turned to the older man. 'We're going to have trouble with this rock, Rob, once we have to blast deeper.'

He pointed to sharp fragments. 'See how it's splitting, Rob? That's where the danger lies, due to ricocheting. You'll have to take care with your next charges.'

Rob Stewart frowned. 'Are you telling me that I don't know my job, Shaun?'

Just when he felt he was making headway with his old friend, Shaun realised he had not handled this point very diplomatically. Looking up, he watched Rob's lips tighten.

The Irishman sighed. 'No, I'm not Rob. You're one of the best tunnellers I know. It's just that this rock will behave differently from any you've worked before.'

'Will it be all right if I tell the men to start clearing up?' the older man asked sharply.

'Of course! We must see how things are farther in. Now I'm afraid I have to leave you for a bit. I've to report back to the boss. He needs me on hand to help with answering the guests' questions.'

Beth became aware that Alec was approaching from the far side of the marquee with plates of food for Bridget and herself.

'I don't know about you two, but all this fresh air has given me an appetite,' he said as he reached them.

Silently, Beth took the plate. She could see Shaun at the entrance to the marquee talking to Robert McAlpine, but every few moments he seemed to look in her direction.

Just then Alec steered the two nurses towards the far corner of the tent where a table had been set up for them.

At the same moment, the Irishman began heading her way. As the party from the hospital sat down at the table, Shaun appeared to change his mind and returned the way he had come.

Beth felt strangely disappointed.

'Your doctor's nice, isn't he?' Bridget whispered as she watched the tall surgeon return to the buffet table to collect food for himself. 'Tell me, now, do I sense something special between you two?'

If nothing else, Nurse O'Malley was forthright, Beth thought.

'Please, Bridget, keep your voice down,' she begged.

'Why, I do believe you're blushing, Sister,' the other girl teased.

When Alec returned, Bridget picked up her plate, and leaned across to whisper in Beth's ear. 'Well, I'll not play gooseberry. I'll just see if I can find someone to chat with myself.'

It had been a strange morning and it had

left Beth feeling unsettled. She suddenly realised that in all the years her father had worked in tunnels, she'd never really seen him in action, nor indeed, how much danger was involved in an operation.

It was whilst standing at a safe distance, first-aid kit and stretcher at the ready, that the enormity of the situation hit her. Now, the thought of a tunnel accident happening made her blood run cold.

'Beth, I'm truly sorry.' Alec Buller's voice broke into her thoughts.

For a dreadful moment, she thought the worst, and began trembling.

'You said you were sorry,' she stammered. 'Tell me, please, has something happened to my father?'

Alec looked at her blankly. 'There's nothing wrong,' he assured her. 'It's Nolan…' Leaning forward, he placed his cupped hand under her chin and forced her to look at him. 'Surely you know what I'm speaking of, Beth. That night you went fishing with the fellow, I acted like some jealous fool. I realise now that you must have had your reasons.'

'I suppose we both spoke hastily, Alec, and yes, I did have a very good reason for seeing Shaun on his own that night. He was worried…'

'About what?' Alec asked. 'Surely you can confide in me?'

She hesitated for a long moment. 'It was personal, Alec, but I daresay I should tell you, since it was you he really wanted to speak to in the first place,' she explained. 'He was calling at the hospital almost every day, wanting to know when you were to arrive. As it happens, Shaun comes from the same part of Ireland as Bridget O'Malley, and she had already told me a little about his past. Anyway, when you had still not arrived, he decided that perhaps I could help,' she continued.

'Beth, perhaps you should start from the beginning,' Alec prompted.

'Yes,' she agreed, 'perhaps that would be best.'

'Quite a tale,' Alec remarked with a sigh when she finished. 'The man does appear to have had his troubles, and it's obvious he's afraid his child may have contracted tuberculosis. Still, from all you've told me about the diagnosis, the child could just as easily have whooping-cough. You did right to suggest a second opinion. I would have done exactly the same,' he complimented her.

Beth's world was slowly righting itself. She was discussing a case with a valued colleague, someone whose advice she trusted.

'There's one thing, Alec,' she suddenly remembered. 'If you should see Shaun, promise you won't say anything about this

159

child being his own daughter. You see, he was speaking hypothetically...'

The man opposite threw back his head and laughed. 'What a tangled web we weave, indeed. But, of course I'll honour your confidence.'

'It should help when the railway runs past our place,' Alec commented as the hospital party began their return journey to Lochailort. 'This is not the most comfortable way to travel.'

The carriage taking them back to Lochailort was using a temporary track.

Bridget, huddled in one corner, seemed unfamiliarly quiet.

'Is something troubling you, Bridget?' Beth asked gently.

The Irish girl looked glum. 'I should learn to hold my tongue,' she admitted. 'I spoke just too bluntly to one of the guests about the navvies' wages. He warned me I should watch what I said, and that he had friends in high places.'

Beth decided to change the subject. 'How's your brother, Bridget? Is his head wound healing up all right?'

'Oh, he's as right as rain,' she replied. 'It will take more than a knock on a door lintel to put him out of action.' The nurse became silent once more, staring at the hills.

'I was just wondering, Doctor?' Bridget

ventured eventually, her freckled face still serious. 'I don't suppose you will be needing a handyman about the hospital? Someone permanent, to look after the boiler and keep the garden tidy? Our Bryan is very good with his hands. I see they have to send odd-job men up from the camp to keep things running at the moment.'

Alec stroked his chin thoughtfully. 'I suppose there might be, Nurse O'Malley, but it would be up to the contractor. And, of course, there's the matter of accommodation,' he pointed out.

Bridget's face brightened. 'Well now, I've thought about that, too,' she said eagerly. 'There's a cottage next to the hospital.'

Beth held her breath, wondering how Alec was going to extricate himself from this plan. The house Bridget mentioned was the same one Alec had felt could be converted into married quarters. She watched him bite his lip then look towards her for help. Quickly she averted her gaze. This was a problem only Alec could solve. She listened to his reply in dismay.

'I'll think about it, Nurse, but as I say, it's not up to me. That house is company property,' he reminded the Irish girl.

Beth remained silent for the rest of the journey. Only once did their eyes meet and Alec gave her a pleading look, but she had no sympathy for his lack of moral courage.

Working alongside him in an operating theatre, she could admire his confidence and natural ability. On those occasions he knew exactly what to do. It was only when it came to matters of the heart that he seemed to lack commitment.

Beth's thoughts were interrupted by the sounds of another vehicle gaining on them. A man dressed in tunnel workers' clothes was waving his arms in the air, attempting to attract their attention. Their own driver, realising what was happening, brought his team of animals to a halt and jumped down on to the track.

'There's been a rockfall at the tunnel!' the man gasped breathlessly. 'It happened when the men went in to clear up. Three men are trapped along with our assistant foreman.'

Alec Buller took charge of the situation immediately. 'The assistant foreman, you say?'

The new arrival nodded. 'Ay – Mr Stewart,' he confirmed. 'He was inside with us while we were removing rock and it happened without warning. The roof seemed to cave in. We had to run for our lives, sir. Then Mr Stewart went back when he discovered the ganger was still inside, and there was another fall.'

Beth gasped. 'Father...' She bowed her head and silently began to pray as she felt

Alec Buller's arm around her shoulders. She clutched at him, fear in her face. 'I must get to Father!' she insisted, keeping her voice steady with an effort.

Alec turned to their driver. 'How fast can you get us back to Corpach?'

The man touched his cap. 'Just as soon as I water the beast, sir. I won't waste a second,' he assured the doctor.

'Good man!' Alec turned back to Beth, automatically taking charge of the situation. 'Now here's what we're going to do, Beth. All three of us will return to Corpach, but we must take our instructions from the rescue team. When we arrive, you and Bridget had better lay out the bandages and so on in the ambulance. Let's pray it's still at the site.'

The driver finished watering the horses, and turned the carriage round.

Huddled in her corner, Beth stared unseeingly as they moved forward, glad that Alec and Bridget didn't attempt to speak to her but left her with her anguished thoughts.

At the scene there hung in the air an atmosphere of gloom. Men lowered their voices as they saw the hospital party arrive as close to the rock-fall as was thought safe.

'What's happening in there?' Alec demanded urgently.

Men had formed themselves into a human chain and were passing boulders carefully from one to the next.

'It's a delicate operation, sir,' a tall ganger explained. 'We can't take the chance of another rock-fall. Mr Nolan's inside right now, supervising. What I don't understand is why there has been no contact from–'

'Hush!' Alec nodded in Beth's direction as she picked her way towards them. 'Mr Stewart is the nurse's father.'

'Where's Shaun Nolan?' Beth demanded as she arrived. 'He should never have allowed this to happen!'

The ganger frowned. 'Wasn't anyone's fault, miss. I heard the boss warn Rob about that roof just minutes before we started to clear up.'

'Come back to the ambulance,' Alec urged. 'I'll try to discover what's going on.'

Beth wrenched herself from him, then ran towards the huge gash in the rock where the main body of rescue workers was sited.

'Keep back, miss.' The warning came from the ganger who had spoken to them earlier. 'This is no place for you.'

Ignoring his words, Beth forced her way to the front. It was then that she saw Shaun Nolan working at the centre of the rock-fall. He was in his shirtsleeves and wielded a short-handled pick.

Every now and then he would hold a hand up for silence, tap four times on the rock-face, then wait.

As he turned to consult with his men, he

caught sight of her and frowned. As he walked towards her, she saw that his face was covered in grime.

'Beth! You can't stay here!' he said urgently. 'Don't you realise you're holding up the rescue? I know how you must be feeling, but I'll get your father out of there, I promise you.'

'How can you possibly know how I feel, and why are they working so slowly?' she retorted, so strung up with worry that she didn't recognise the concern in his voice.

Almost forcefully, Shaun led her away from the danger area.

'We can't take the chance of another fall,' he explained. 'Please, Beth, this is the best way. Trust me, I beg you. I realise just how you must be feeling. I admire and respect, yes, and love your father ... and if you'll give me a chance I'll bring him out.'

Shaun looked up and caught sight of Alec Buller. 'Please keep Beth out of here, will you?' He lowered his voice. 'It's pretty dangerous back there at the moment.' All the old rivalry and animosity between the two men had melted in their shared anxiety.

'Let me know if I can help,' Alec urged. 'I'm quite slim and can get through most narrow spaces. If you can find a way to the trapped men they may need urgent medical attention.'

Shaun raised a hand wearily in acknowledgement. 'I'll do that, believe me, but I must get back now,' he apologised.

Beth was so deeply shocked she was unaware she was being led back to the ambulance. It was only when Bridget thrust a cup of hot tea into her hands that she realised where she was.

'We'll get your father out of there, miss,' said the tall ganger who had met them on their arrival. He seemed to be taking a personal interest in Beth. 'One of the best, is Rob Stewart,' he added. 'Won't ask a man to do anything he's not prepared to attempt himself.'

From inside the tunnel, rescue activity halted once more, and Beth could hear the sound of metal clanging on rock, then silence once more as men waited. She held her breath. A moment later the work began again.

It was some time later that the onlookers outside became aware of a buzz of excitement amongst the rescue workers. Then came the echoing sound of a man's voice as he called for complete silence.

Moments later, a dust-covered rescuer came hurrying across to the hospital party.

'Somebody has answered our signal!' he told the three of them. 'With a bit of luck, we'll get them out soon.'

Working slowly, with painstaking care, the

rescue workers removed the last of the rocks blocking the tunnel, aware that one false move would not only be disastrous for the trapped men, but also for themselves.

At one point in the rescue, the hospital party learned Shaun Nolan had to use his own body like a shield, as one by one, the trapped men were dragged to safety.

Rob Stewart was the last to appear, his right leg gashed and bleeding, but otherwise looking none the worse for his ordeal.

One man had sustained head injuries and Alec took over, supervising stretchering him off to the ambulance, where Bridget was administering first-aid to lesser injuries.

Then Alec turned to Beth. 'Your place is with your father,' he urged her. 'I can manage without you at the moment.'

She ran across the rough ground and threw herself into Rob Stewart's arms.

'Och, lass, look at your pretty uniform. It's all stour!' he declared.

She laughed through her tears of relief. 'What's wrong with a bit of stour, Dad? Oh, I'm so glad to see you. I thought for a bit—'

Rob grew serious. 'Ay, lass, and so did I,' he admitted. 'Tell me, where's Shaun? I must thank him for what he did back there. You should have seen him, Beth. He shored up that opening long enough for us all to get through, then had to jump for it himself as the roof fell in.'

Guiltily, Beth turned and caught sight of Shaun sitting at the mouth of the tunnel, his head in his hands.

'Go to him, lass. See if the lad's all right,' Rob Stewart said quietly.

As Rob limped painfully towards the ambulance, Beth did as she was bid. She could see that the Irishman was also in some pain as he sat up and gingerly eased the shirt on his shoulders.

'Here, let me,' she offered. Gently, she examined the bruises and lacerations across his shoulders. As he winced, Beth signalled to Alec.

'I think you should take a look at Shaun, please.'

Alec hurried across and examined the foreman carefully.

'Looks like muscle damage. We'll make you a bit more comfortable, shall we?'

Beth began to fasten a wide bandage across Shaun's shoulder and chest for support. As she did so, she looked him straight in the eye.

'Thanks, Shaun,' she told him softly. 'I heard what you did back there.'

He gave her a weary smile. 'We didn't have a prop handy, Beth, and I've a good strong back!' he declared. Shakily, he rose to his feet and began to walk towards the ambulance where he spoke to Rob.

Beth watched them solemnly shake hands.

It Was All Over

It was almost Christmas, and hard weather had set into the West Highlands. All day long, a biting wind seemed to blow in from the sea, and the mountains were shrouded in snow. Drifts covered the newly-laid railway tracks as work ground to a halt. Work also halted in the tunnel at Corpach while Robert McAlpine, the contractor, took expert advice.

One good thing about the temporary halt in building was that Rob and Shaun had an opportunity to recuperate, the latter having been detained for observation in the infirmary at Fort William. Rob's leg injury had required stitching but, since he lived in the town, he was allowed home. One of the trapped tunnelmen had been detained with delayed concussion, and two others were released after treatment.

Shaun Nolan's shoulders, which had been injured by the rocks, were taking longer to respond to treatment.

He was still in some pain when, on a visit to see him, Rob Stewart suggested, 'Why don't you stay at our house, Shaun, until you get your strength back? You could spend

Christmas with the family and perhaps attend the christening of our first grandchild.'

The Irishman's first response was delight, then his face fell. 'But surely it's a family thing, Rob?' he queried.

Rob shook his head. 'Man, if you'd not risked your life back at the tunnel, my family would be fatherless today!'

Since injuries at the Lochailort Hospital had lessened because of the halt in work, Beth was allowed to travel home to Fort William to attend the family celebrations.

'I'll try to come down for the christening day,' Alec promised, 'but it will depend on how busy we are.'

'That's all right,' Beth assured him. 'I know you'll try.'

Bridget looked rather subdued as Beth said goodbye to her.

'Anything wrong?' the older girl asked tentatively.

The Irish girl's lips quivered. 'It's the first time I've ever been away from home for Christmas,' she admitted.

'You'll have your brother,' Beth comforted her.

'That one! Bryan is anything but a comfort, I can tell you. I'd need to keep him under my eye all day, and that won't be easy with him down at the camp. He's so headstrong, you see. I just wish I could...'

Bridget turned towards Alec Buller. 'You said you were going to find out if that odd-job man's position was available, Doctor.'

'And I did, Nurse O'Malley,' Alec assured her. 'Mr McAlpine says your brother can start with us after the New Year and live in the cottage – provided he's willing to repair it.'

Bridget's face lit up as she shook the doctor's hand enthusiastically.

'Oh, sir, you won't regret this, I promise you!' she exclaimed.

Beth shared in the younger nurse's delight, but as she looked towards Alec Buller, she noticed that he couldn't meet her eye. So much for his talk about the cottage being suitable for a married couple...

The Stewarts' house was crowded with relatives and friends who'd come from far and near to celebrate young Catherine's christening.

Janet had been cooking for days, and the Christmas table sagged under the weight of her efforts.

From his favourite seat by the chimney, Fergus McCallum watched the celebrations. Saul, his eldest son, whose boat lay in the harbour at this moment, had arrived in time for the christening. Afterwards, Saul mentioned to the company that he intended taking his father back home to Mallaig.

'It was peace, perfect peace with him away, I can tell you, but I suppose it's not the same without him. He's sailing back with me on the first tide tomorrow.'

Shaun decided to take a short stroll through the Stewarts' garden, and Beth joined him. Today, the place had a magical look about it. Hedges were tinselled with the frost and icicles hung like candles from pear trees. To Shaun's surprise there were still roses to be seen, pale, cream blooms caught by the cold snap.

They looked at the frozen garden in silence, then Beth broke the spell.

'Dad had to take a red-hot poker today to loosen leeks from the ground, so Mum could have them for her soup pot.'

'She's still a grand cook,' Shaun agreed, and turned to gaze at Beth wistfully. 'I'd almost forgotten what it felt like to be part of a family gathering like this. The christening service was lovely, wasn't it?'

Beth nodded, remembering the moment when she stood at the font with her precious godchild, who was wearing the robe which Will and she had both worn in turn.

'There's something important I must tell you. It's about Julie,' he said bluntly. 'You know – the child I told you about that night on the loch?'

He looked her in the eye. 'Julie's my own

172

daughter, Beth. Being the person you are, I imagine you already suspected that. My wife, Rosa, died having her.'

'Yes, I knew that, Shaun. Some of it was already in your medical records,' she explained.

'And I suppose the rest was filled in by Bridget O'Malley!'

They walked down the icy path. Beth pulling the collar of her jacket up around her chin.

'It was seeing young Catherine that brought it all back,' Shaun continued. 'When Julie was baptised I left everything to my folk. I didn't have the heart to take part. You might say, I … I took the coward's way out – neglected my responsibility.'

'I don't believe that for one moment. Everyone has their own way of grieving, and it takes time to come to terms with the loss. I'm sure your parents realised that, too,' Beth said gently.

'But you don't understand, Beth!' he protested. 'I caused my wife's death.'

Beth stopped in her tracks. 'Look, I think you'd better tell me everything. Let's go to Dad's potting-shed,' she suggested. 'It will be warmer in there.'

But now that the floodgates had opened for Shaun, he couldn't wait for another moment. He began to give way to all the pent-up emotions and doubts which had caused him such anguish.

'If I hadn't taken Rosa away from a warm climate, Beth, and dragged her halfway across the world because of my work, then she might have been alive today,' he went on, bitterness in his voice. 'She'd tuberculosis, you know. That's why I was so worried about little Julie when Mam wrote and said she was poorly.'

Beth gasped, and Shaun turned quickly to her.

'She's going to be all right. The doctor confirmed that Julie has whooping-cough. She'll need careful nursing, of course, but thank goodness for your advice, Beth,' he finished, his voice unsteady.

As she looked up at him, Beth noticed tears trickling down his tanned cheeks. This man, who had saved her father's life a few days before, with no thought for his own safety, had reached his breaking-point.

She drew closer to him, held his hand in hers and soothed him.

'Weep away, Shaun. You've been bottling things up for too long,' she comforted him.

They'd reached the shed where her father kept his vegetables. Onions hung on strings from the rafters and boxes were stacked against the wall. Vegetables set in straw had been stored to see the household through the cold months.

'Here, Shaun, this was our sofa in the parlour when you lodged with us, remember? Sit down and tell me everything.'

They sat for almost an hour as Shaun spoke of Rosa, their life together, and of the great emptiness her death had left in his life.

Beth said very little, only prompting him gently now and then.

At last he regained his composure. 'Oh, Beth,' he said with a shaky smile. 'What must you think of me? I've never spoken like this to anyone before.'

He gazed into her dark eyes and recognised sympathy – or was there something more? Suddenly, he reached forward and drew Beth towards him. To his joy, she did not draw back. When his lips met hers, she seemed ready to respond.

Shaun sat back and stared at Beth. 'I'm sorry, Beth. Forgive me. I'd no right to–' he began haltingly.

She touched his lips with two fingers. 'Hush!' she said, before getting to her feet and offering Shaun both her hands.

'We'll go back to the house now,' she told him. 'Mother will be wondering where we are.'

They had all but reached the back door when Shaun halted in his tracks. 'I forgot to tell you, Beth. I'm going home tomorrow to Ireland. The doctor at the infirmary says I won't be able to work for at least a fortnight, so I'm taking the opportunity to see Julie.'

Beth nodded. 'That's an excellent idea, Shaun.' But as she spoke the words, she felt a pang of disappointment. She was going to miss Shaun – he had suddenly become very important to her.

Next morning the Stewart household seemed very subdued. Beth watched Fergus McCallum eat his last breakfast cooked by Janet's capable hands.

'You're not looking for a job as a house-keeper, by any chance?' he asked half-jokingly.

'Indeed she's not!' Rob Stewart replied for his wife. 'Go and hire yourself a house-keeper, Fergus, and remember what I said about Mhairi. She's not to be your skivvy any more. That lass will have enough on her hands with young Catherine to take care of when she goes home.'

'All right, all right! You've made your point, Rob.'

Later, Beth and her father saw Shaun off on the train that would take him to the ferry for his long journey back to Ireland.

'You'll come to see me as soon as you're fit,' Rob said briskly. 'There's a lot we have to talk about before we do any more tunnel work.'

It was the nearest Beth's father would ever get to admitting that there were things Shaun could teach him about new methods, but he was learning.

As Rob boarded the train to put Shaun's luggage on the rack, the Irishman turned towards Beth.

'Will you want me back, too, little one?' he asked with a new intensity.

'Come back soon, Shaun,' was all she would say.

Rob reappeared on the platform, and they waved until the train was out of sight.

'I'm going to miss that fellow,' Rob told his daughter.

She had to bite her tongue to prevent herself replying, 'And so will I, Father, so will I.'

The house seemed so empty when father and daughter returned. Janet was sweeping around the kitchen with her broom, and Mhairi was feeding little Catherine. It was a homely scene, and Beth and her mother exchanged glances. They realised that as soon as Catherine was fit to travel, Mhairi, too, would be leaving for Mallaig.

'I'm going to miss Mhairi so much,' Janet said sadly. 'She sort of made up for you leaving home, Beth.'

It was the first time Beth had heard her mother speak like this. She was always such a sensible person, happiest when busy running her own life, caught up with town affairs, keeping her house spotless.

Beth looked closer. She noticed lines in

her mother's face that had not been there before.

Now, well into her sixties, Janet Stewart moved more slowly and once, when she bent to shovel up dust, Beth noticed her wince.

'Are you all right, Mother?'

'Of course I am, love. Just a bit tired after all our celebrations.'

Beth wasn't convinced and later spoke to her sister-in-law.

'I've thought that she looked a bit weary lately,' Mhairi agreed. 'She's been doing too much, I suppose. Still, when we go, she should be able to rest more.'

Yes, Beth thought, she'll have the whole house to herself once Father starts to work farther up the line. The thought did little to reassure her.

When she returned to Lochailort, Beth realised there had been several changes in her absence. For one thing, the boiler was working perfectly. Bryan O'Malley, having settled himself into his new job, was proving his worth. What caught Beth's attention immediately was a lantern in the window of the cottage at the end of the hospital road. In his spare time, it seemed, Bryan had made a start on its re-furbishing.

'I hear they've started work on the viaduct at Glenfinnan,' Alec Buller announced as they ate supper together. 'Perhaps we could take a ride out there one day? They say it's going to be quite an undertaking.'

'Perhaps,' Beth agreed.

She had the feeling Alec didn't want to be alone with her in case she mentioned the possibility of a future together.

'How did the christening go?' he asked.

Once more, Beth gave the briefest of replies.

'Everything went well, Alec. Sorry you couldn't be there.'

The doctor bit his lip. 'Well, Beth, someone had to hold the fort. If Bridget were here she would tell you how busy we were.'

'Where is Bridget, by the way?'

Alec's face flushed. 'She's helping her brother to clear out the cottage, I believe,' he said, clearing his throat.

'Ah yes, the cottage. So Bryan is to occupy it after all?'

Alec cleared his throat again. 'It does seem the most sensible solution, Beth, don't you agree? I mean, we don't have accommodation for him here at the hospital…'

'I'm sure you're right, Alec. It's a sensible solution, as you say.'

The relief on his face was almost amusing. Beth rose from the table and swept upstairs to her room. She crossed to the window and threw it open. From the cottage down the road she could hear Bridget's deep, contralto voice singing, and the accompanying chorus being taken up by her brother.

At least someone had found a solution to her immediate problem. Bridget O'Malley might seem unworldly, but she had a way of getting things done to her own satisfaction.

The winter snows had all but disappeared from the moorland around Lochailort. Only the mountains remained shrouded.

During the past months, Beth had experienced the full force of a Highland winter, with snowdrifts and icicles outdoors while inside the small hospital, heaters barely coped with the low temperatures.

But it was not just the elements outside which had left Beth feeling raw. Inside the small hospital, working beside Alec Buller, the atmosphere there had grown distinctly cool, too.

With only three personnel on the medical team, each one had been prepared to cope with whatever presented itself. Only the day before, Alec was called down to attend an emergency at the camp, to discover his patient was an injured cart-horse.

When he returned to the hospital, he shook his head. 'And that's why I studied surgery,' he mused sarcastically.

Bridget, who was binding up a plate-layer's thumb, looked up. 'Didn't you manage to save the poor beast then, Doctor?'

He nodded wryly. 'Oh, yes, Nurse O'Malley. It was one of the best pieces of needlework I've done since I arrived!'

Beth listened to his conversation as she wrote in her day-book. She'd suspected for some time now that Alec was becoming more and more disillusioned by the camp hospital. What did he want, she asked herself, a major disaster?

As far as she was concerned, Beth could feel only relief that there had not been too many serious accident victims brought in to them, for Alec was not the only one who'd come to realise they had been equipped to deal with only minor emergencies.

Since the weather had cleared, work on the building of the extension to Mallaig was now taking place at a furious pace, particularly at the site of the Glenfinnan viaduct. Rails connecting this with the main line were being laid as the work progressed. Soon, Beth's father confided on her last visit home, she would be able to ride back and forth by train to Fort William, instead of using the time-consuming series of ferries and carts or coaches.

Just as the hospital staff sat down to lunch, news came that there had been an accident near the viaduct and an ambulance was needed.

Beth looked across the table. 'You'll be happy now, I suppose?' she said dryly.

Alec ignored this sarcasm. He swallowed his last mouthful and jumped to his feet. 'We'd better be going, Sister.'

He turned to Bridget a little patronisingly. 'I take it I can leave you in charge here, Nurse O'Malley?'

The Irish girl's brows rose, but her reply was calm. 'Of course, sir. I'll see that everything runs smoothly.'

Beth sighed. The situation between Alec and herself was uncomfortable, but it was wrong of him to take it out on Bridget. She turned to the Irish girl and gave last-minute instructions, then put on her cape and bonnet.

They made their way as fast as the rough track would allow, while the man at the reins of the horse-driven ambulance told them what he knew about the accident. The injured plate-layer had been trapped by falling metal as it was being unloaded from a wagon.

The journey to the site would take more than an hour, but there was to be little conversation between doctor and nurse during this time, other than the odd remark made by the driver. The embarrassing silence made Beth retreat into the corner of her seat and immerse herself in private thoughts.

She found herself watching Alec covertly. He'd changed over the last months. He rarely smiled now when they were together.

Their driver appeared to be making heavy weather of the journey. The track was riddled with ruts and displaced boulders.

'Do you know how badly the man is injured?' Beth asked.

'Couldn't really say, Sister. The foreman said his leg seemed caught beneath a pile of rails.'

'We'll make our own diagnosis on the site, Sister,' Alec reproved her, turning away after he spoke.

At last the journey ended. Straight ahead of them, Beth and Alec could see a group of workmen gathered near a siding where sections of rail were being unloaded from a wagon.

'Over here!' an anxious ganger called. Releasing the injured workman was a delicate operation, the man explained. Lengths of iron rail were being carefully removed so that the doctor could examine the injured man in more detail.

When enough space had been cleared, Alec Buller wriggled under the wagon. Beth felt a stirring of pride. She'd always admired the way he never hesitated when it came to an emergency like this. Perhaps it had been what had first attracted her.

He reappeared from under the wagon, his

hair streaked grey with dust, and signalled for Beth to approach.

'It's not as bad as I first imagined,' he told her, keeping his voice down. 'I think it's only the man's foot that's trapped. Can you pass me my bag, please?'

She did so, and he gave a sedative to the injured workman who was now beginning to regain consciousness.

'That's all we can do until he's free,' Alec said. 'We'll just have to pack rugs around him and wait.'

It took almost an hour to free their patient. Alec walked up and down impatiently.

Once, however, he stopped by Beth's side. 'Where's your Irishman today, then?' he demanded.

'If you mean Shaun Nolan,' Beth replied evenly, 'I believe he's working at Glenfinnan, and for your information he is not my Irishman. We are friends.'

'If you say so, Sister.'

She recognised derision in his tone and her cheeks flamed. She realised now that most of Alec's coolness towards her was because of Shaun. It was true that she saw a fair bit of the Irish foreman, but in fact, their meetings were due more to Shaun's renewed friendship with her father.

When Shaun had returned after his convalescence in Ireland, after being injured rescuing Rob in a rock-fall, there had been much work to catch up with and he'd needed to attend to Company business at Fort William. On those occasions, Rob Stewart had insisted on Shaun staying at the Stewart cottage. These visits occasionally coincided with Beth's free weekends.

That she felt attracted towards Shaun was undeniable, otherwise why did her heart race whenever she saw him? For Shaun, there had been only one love in his life, and that was Rosa. No other woman could ever take the place of his late wife...

'We've got him free, Doctor.' The ganger came hurrying across, and Beth was jerked out of her reverie. 'Would you examine him before we try to get him out of there?'

Once again Alec hurried to the spot, Beth by his side this time. After they'd examined the injured workman, they looked at one another.

Beth bit her lip. This man's career as a plate-layer on the line was over. The foot was very badly crushed.

Gently, four workmen carried him by stretcher to the ambulance.

'Poor devil!' Alec murmured to Beth.

'The journey back isn't going to help,' Beth admitted sadly. 'I think I'll sit in the back with him. At least I can save him from being jostled about too much.'

'We both will.' Alec nodded.

The journey back to the hospital began, their attentions now caught up in a joint effort to save the worker further injury.

Afterwards, the hospital staff discussed the situation.

'It was impossible,' Alec declared. 'If I'd had the man in my old hospital in Glasgow, under better conditions, I could have saved that foot.'

'You did everything you could,' Bridget maintained stoutly, and Beth nodded. All three had worked continuously in theatre, but to no avail. She could sense Alec's frustration and attempted to comfort him.

'We can only do our best, in the circumstances,' she reminded him. 'We can't work miracles.'

He swung round angrily. 'You don't see, do you? I might have worked that miracle you speak of if I'd had the right equipment. This place is beginning to depress me!' he exclaimed.

He turned on his heel and left the two nurses gazing at one another.

'Poor man! He's really upset!' Bridget bit her lip. 'I can understand, I suppose. He's such a brilliant surgeon, but he'll never make a name for himself here.'

Beth shook her head impatiently. 'Why is it so important for Alec Buller to make a name for himself!' she demanded. 'We're here to do a job, and we can only do it to the best of our abilities. If Alec is determined to become a hero, then he'll have to do it elsewhere.'

The Irish girl seemed taken aback. 'I was only saying–'

'Yes,' Beth snapped. 'I know what you were saying, Bridget. Don't you think I felt disappointed, too? The poor man in that bed out there will have to live the rest of his life with disappointment, but he's still alive. Isn't that something to be thankful for?'

She vowed that she would do all she could to help him rebuild his life. As she wheeled around, she became aware that Alec Buller had returned to the staff-room, and must have heard her scathing remarks.

Later Beth went outside for a breath of fresh air. The day had been long and frustrating. Tonight, the sky was almost indigo blue. Clouds moved swiftly overhead, occasionally blotting out the new moon, a mere sliver of gold.

The only sound came from a burn to her right as it tumbled noisily over weathered boulders.

'I'm sorry for the outburst.' Alec had come up silently behind her and laid a hand on her shoulder.

She drew away instantly and heard his harsh intake of breath.

'Can't I do anything right nowadays, Beth – even apologise? Once, I used to feel we two were a pair, that there was a future somewhere ahead for us together. That was why I agreed to come to this wild outpost in the first place.'

The girl gasped.

'Was that really the reason you came here?' she asked with a tremor in her voice.

He swung her round to face him. 'Deny it if you will, Beth, but there was something between us,' he insisted. 'I could feel it whenever we were together.'

She nodded. 'I don't deny it, but, Alec, what did you do about it? I remember only too well that first day we came up here, and you told me about that house over there – how it would make good married quarters. Yet you didn't hesitate to let Bryan O'Malley have it instead. I don't think you were ever ready to make a proper commitment. It was just some pipe-dream,' she said sadly.

The man beside her whistled in the darkness. 'So that's what this has all been about! You really did want to settle down, Beth. But can't you see it from my point of view?

'This isn't the place for us, not on any permanent basis. I never intended it to be so,' he explained.

'When we first came here, I expected to

find a post where I could work to my full potential. I even wrote a letter to my old professor asking him to keep his ear to the ground for any likely opportunities,' he told her.

'Beth, it was only to be a matter of time, then I could have found us a proper home. This was merely a stop-gap. Surely you realised that?'

She couldn't trust herself to speak.

'Beth, if it's commitment you want, will this do?' He pulled her into his arms, and his lips were hard and demanding.

'Promise me one thing, Beth,' Alec begged when she struggled out of his embrace. 'Say you'll marry me as soon as I can find a proper posting...'

'Alec!' she broke in. 'Listen to yourself! It's all about *you* – how *you* feel about your work, where *your* life should be taking you. Don't I matter at all? How I feel? Where I want to live? If you search your heart, you'll recognise that I come pretty far down your list of priorities.'

If she had slapped his face, Alec Buller could not have looked more shocked.

'That's not true, Beth, and you know it,' he protested. 'I've always loved you, but a man has to be the breadwinner and make the decisions. You're a first-class nurse, but when we marry I would want you to forget about that – I'd want you at home.

'Perhaps I've never been able to put it into the words you want to hear, and I'll never have the charm of Nolan, who can so obviously turn your head. Oh yes, Beth, I'm not blind,' he told her. 'I see how you look when he's around.'

Was she really so transparent, Beth wondered. Yet if he were so observant, Alec must have noticed there had been no response from Shaun Nolan...

'I'm sorry, Alec,' she said sadly. 'Some day you'll meet a girl who is exactly right for you, one who will share all your dreams and fall in with whatever plans you make, but I'm not the person for you. I don't believe I ever was...'

Beth lay in bed that night staring up through the skylight window, her mind in torment.

At last, Alec Buller had asked her to marry him – something she'd longed for him to do when they'd been close. Now that he had done so, and she had refused, it was all over.

Perhaps she'd never really been as ambitious as Alec, she mused. To her, the thought of working at the new camp hospital, to be part of the great railway project her father had spoken of for years, was excitement enough.

A Sad Homecoming

A new working relationship seemed to grow between Alec and Beth. They concentrated upon making the new hospital as efficient as possible.

Nowadays, Bridget O'Malley brought the only light relief to Beth's rather empty life at Lochailort. The Irish girl's life seemed uncomplicated, and she appeared eternally grateful for its smooth running.

'This was the best thing that could ever have happened to Bryan and me,' she said with satisfaction one day.

Beth looked up curiously. 'What's that, Bridget?'

'Why, me getting this steady job, and our Bryan setting himself up in that cottage along the road. You know he's turning into quite a homemaker,' the Irish girl continued. 'Have you seen the garden?'

Beth shook her head. She was ashamed to admit that she had not given much thought to Bryan O'Malley recently, so caught up had she become in her own personal troubles, yet she had to admit the young man was proving a good worker.

'He's got a girl, you know,' Bridget

mentioned shyly.

Beth raised her eyebrows. 'A girl? How did he manage that in such a remote place?' she asked.

'Her father is station-master down the line a bit, and Bryan met her when he was buying provisions in Fort William,' Bridget explained. 'He's bringing her to meet me at the weekend, and he asked me if you'd like to come over for a meal with us.'

'Oh no, Bridget, I don't really think–' Beth began.

'Say you'll come, won't you? The boy's desperate to gain her approval.'

'But why me?' Beth argued.

The Irish girl grinned. 'Sure, he thinks that you're the most respectable person he knows, not scatty like me.'

The comparison was intended to be a compliment, but Beth's confidence took another knock. Bridget was obviously being kind, but was she really as dull as Bryan saw her?

'All right,' she agreed at last. 'I'll come.'

As it turned out it was a really pleasant evening. Bryan was quite an expert on the tin whistle and played merry jigs for them. Everyone was coaxed into singing a song, accompanied by Bryan on the whistle, then Bridget entertained them by relating hilarious tales of their life in Ireland.

Bryan's girl turned out to be Morag Grey,

who worked for the large bakery in Fort William which also supplied provisions to the camp shops.

'I know your mother, Beth,' Morag told her. 'She often comes into the shop.'

Beth brightened. 'I haven't been home for weeks,' she said. 'How was she looking, Morag?'

The girl hesitated before replying. 'As a matter of fact, I thought she seemed a bit tired the last time we spoke. She said she had been to see her doctor.'

Beth leaned forward. 'Her doctor? That's not like Mum at all?'

Supper turned out to be homely fare, soda bread and a selection of farm cheese and ginger preserve which Mrs O'Malley had sent in a parcel from Ireland.

After supper, Morag insisted that it was time she left. Bryan looked the picture of disappointment, but insisted upon escorting her.

'She seems a nice girl,' Beth said.

Bridget nodded. 'I like her, too. I hope they hit it off together.'

Beth shared her hopes. It was nice to see some lives running smoothly.

'I think I'll head back, too, Bridget,' she decided.

The Irish nurse nodded absent-mindedly. 'I'll just tidy up here a bit. I'll be over shortly,' she promised.

As she neared the hospital, Beth could see Alec Buller sitting at the window of his office. Although there were no in-patients, he'd refused Bridget's invitation to join them for supper, making the excuse that he had letters to write. He must have heard the sound of her feet on the gravel for as she reached his door, it opened.

'Did you have a good time?' he asked.

She nodded. 'It made a nice change. You should have come, Alec.'

He looked at her hesitantly. 'Won't you come into the office, Beth? I've something to tell you.' His face looked serious and she followed him into the room.

'I've had a letter, Beth, from my old professor,' he began. 'I've been offered a job in Glasgow. It won't be starting for another month, so I'll not be leaving you all in the lurch, but I just thought you should know.'

She chose her words carefully. 'Congratulations, Alec. I hope this is what you really want.'

'I'll be able to concentrate purely on surgery,' he said with enthusiasm.

Beth held out her hands, and he took them in his own.

'There's still time to—'

She knew what he was about to say, and forestalled him.

'I don't think so, Alec. I'm afraid it will have to be the parting of the ways, but I trust we can remain friends?'

The glimmer of hope which she had read in his eyes died, and he released her.

'Of course, Beth. You know I'll always remember you.'

As she went upstairs to her bedroom, Beth knew that whatever lay ahead for her, it would not include Alec Buller.

The new resident doctor arrived from Glasgow one month later on a cold, misty morning. Clouds hid from view the tall mountains, and even the loch far below was obliterated. The scene could not have looked particularly inviting to the new arrival.

'I hope it's not always like this, Sister?' he asked.

Beth shook her head. 'Oh, not at all, Doctor. You should see it on a fine day.'

Suddenly, the man's eyes twinkled. 'I'm just teasing. As a matter of fact, I happen to know this part of the country well. Ina – that's my wife – hails from Arisaig. She's been longing to come back home for years.' He thrust out a hand. 'The name's John Robertson, Sister, I hope we are going to have a fruitful working relationship.'

Beth hoped so, too. It would be nice to have things running smoothly once more. She could feel herself warming towards him.

John Robertson revealed that he was nearing retirement. He had come from an extremely busy hospital in the city, and when the railway company offered him a four-year contract, he explained to Beth, he had jumped at the chance.

'I was getting too old for the hectic life of a city casualty ward. Besides, I never got much chance to be with Ina. Right now she's staying with a sister in Arisaig, but we'll soon find a more permanent place.'

He moved into Alec Buller's old room and began to unpack.

There was an air of finality about this. Only the day before, Beth and Bridget had shaken Alec's hand, wished him well in his new appointment and waved as he left.

Beth had decided to give up her weekend off, reasoning it would be unfair to take it during the new doctor's first week.

By midday they'd dealt with twenty new workmen arriving steadily from the camp below. As Beth saw the last one off, Shaun Nolan arrived on horseback. Despite her determination to remain calm, Beth felt a familiar tingle along her spine.

He wasn't working at the Glenfinnan site, but of course he was always moving down the line when any tunnel work was in progress.

'Beth!' he hailed her. 'I've come with a letter from your father.' He thrust it into her hands and Beth tore it open, aware that Shaun's eyes were fixed upon her.

'It's my mother!'

Shaun's arm went immediately around her shoulders. 'I know about it, Beth,' he explained. 'I've just come from the Fort. Rob says it was a heart attack, and the doctor was with her when I left. Believe me, she's in good hands.'

As she read the letter through for a second time, Beth became aware that Shaun was speaking urgently to John Robertson, and that Bridget was hurrying towards her.

Bridget O'Malley had become more than just a working companion this last year. The Irish girl had proved a splendid nurse, inspiring confidence in all their patients. Now it was she who took over.

'Look, Beth, your place is at home right this minute. Dr Robertson and I can handle everything while you're away.'

'Of course, you must go home, Sister,' the doctor agreed after Shaun told him what had happened. 'We'll arrange for some sick leave and I'll put in a request for a temporary replacement, if it will make you feel happier. Get off now, or you may be too late to catch the afternoon coach.'

'Not if Beth rides with me,' Shaun suggested.

Beth found herself being helped into the saddle behind Shaun Nolan. She clasped his waist and he urged the big horse into a gallop.

There had not even been time for her to change her dress, and her nursing cloak billowed behind her as they rode to the inn where the coach was almost ready to leave.

Beth pulled out her father's letter and read it again once they were seated on the coach.

Shaun moved closer as she began to tremble.

Your mother took a bad turn yesterday, Beth, when she was coming home from shopping. The doctor says it's her heart.

Beth thrust the letter back into her pocket and gave a sigh of despair.

Janet Stewart, ill? Beth had always thought of her mother as being so strong and capable. Even when Morag Grey spoke of her mother looking tired, it had not really sunk in, yet she was herself a qualified nurse.

The feeling of guilt grew stronger as the miles disappeared beneath the coach's wheels.

'Please, God, don't let it be serious! Perhaps Father has over-reacted.' She did not realise she had spoken aloud until Shaun drew her close and tried to comfort her.

When Beth and Shaun reached Fort William, the streets were thronged with workmen newly arrived off the train from Glasgow. She'd heard that the company was hiring more men for the viaduct being constructed at Glenfinnan.

Shaun took hold of Beth's hand and led her through the crowds on the pavements. They would take the short path through the cutting, he explained. It would save time.

Time! Why was it so important? Then at last Beth could see the house on the hill, smoke rising from its chimney, an air of normality about it all. Yet Beth felt sure things were anything but normal. A strange, raw feeling was gnawing at her heart and she began to run.

As she pushed the door wide, she could see her father on the stair, ashen-faced.

'Oh, lass, thank God you've come. The doctor's with your mother now.

'Go to her, Beth. She's been calling for you all morning.'

Beth's eyes took a moment to focus as she entered the shadowy room. She became aware of the bulky outline of her father, his entire bearing one of distress. Then her gaze was drawn towards the bed where her mother lay.

Janet Stewart's eyes were closed, but Beth's quick intake of breath caused them to flutter open.

'Oh, lass, you've come,' she murmured, saying the words with an effort.

Beth leaned across the covers to kiss her mother's cheek. She could feel a hard knot tightening inside her, and she needed her years of nursing training to seem calm.

'I came as quickly as I could, Mother. Please try not to speak too much. Take things easy.'

The woman in the bed raised her hand. It was a gesture Beth knew of old.

'No time to take things easy, lass. There are things to be said.' Her voice sounded stronger, and this gave Beth hope.

Janet Stewart lifted her head from the pillow and signalled to her husband to leave the room.

Rob sighed but moved out to the landing.

'That's better. I wanted us to be alone,' Janet explained. 'Rob, poor man, can't cope at times like this. Beth, dear, there's no easy way of saying this. It won't be long now...'

Beth gasped, and her mother's pale face creased into a faint smile.

'I know you're a clever nurse and think that you know all about these things. The doctor keeps assuring me that I'm going to get better but, Beth, I know how I feel,' Janet continued. 'I've run a long race but it's come to the end. Och, don't look like that. I have no regrets...'

As Beth took in what her mother was saying, she was struck speechless.

Janet watched her with unwavering calm.

'It's true, you know. I've had a grand life. I've done most of the things I set out to and there are not many who can say that,' she pointed out.

She paused for a moment as though to collect her thoughts before going on. 'It's you, lass. I'm a bit worried about...'

'Me? Why on earth should–'

From somewhere, Janet Stewart summoned the strength to push herself up. 'Beth, dear,' she began. 'I've had the feeling recently that your life has reached a crossroads. I thought for a while that you might have had a future with Alec Buller. He's a fine young man, in his own way, but I never felt sure that he was right for you – a bit too ambitious, perhaps? Then there's Shaun Nolan. Your father and I both liked him when he stayed with us. Of course, there was that bit of trouble with your dad when Shaun was made tunnel foreman, but that's all been settled.'

Janet Stewart hesitated before going on. 'Beth, I have to ask you this. Could he be the right one? No, don't answer yet. Hear what I have to say. Both your father and I think Shaun is a strong character.'

Beth's hand flew to her mouth, her cheeks burning. She'd no idea that her mother knew so much about her life now that she'd moved away from home.

As if she were reading her thoughts, the

201

woman in the bed smiled.

'You know what they say, dear, the onlooker sees most of the game. It's been the best part of my life, watching my children growing up. But enough of that, there's no time to waste.'

Realising how much this conversation meant to her mother, and reminding herself that every word uttered required an immense effort, Beth leaned forward.

'Yes, of course, Mother, I'm listening,' she promised, putting her ear close to her mother's lips.

For the rest of her life, Beth would remember that one-sided conversation, intended for her ears only, words that shocked at first, because they were so frank and forthright.

Janet Stewart had always been regarded as an organised person. She insisted upon writing down long shopping lists, keeping her household accounts in a battered black book. It had become something of a family joke, but Beth was quite unprepared for the detailed list of instructions with which she was now being issued.

Her mother pointed towards the bedside cabinet.

'I realise you won't remember everything, so I've written it all down. If, when the time comes, you can't remember what I had to say, there are letters in that drawer, one for each of you.

'I know you of old, Beth. You're efficient, and have a habit of taking on responsibility. Perhaps you're not aware of it, lass, but you're a lot like me.'

Janet Stewart was speaking more slowly now, frequently pausing for breath, and although her words were breaking Beth's heart, she nodded to show that she understood.

'I don't mean to blackmail any of you, Beth, or insist that you must carry out my wishes. They're just thoughts I've been gathering together for months. Trouble was, I could never get you all together,' she said with a faint smile. 'Beth, it's my dearest wish that you all succeed in your dreams.'

'Dreams?'

Her mother nodded. 'Ay, lass, dreams. We've always been a family of dreamers, your dad with his railway, Will and the sea...'

'And me?'

The elderly woman's expression was remote as she responded.

'Yes, Beth, you! You've had a few dreams in the past, but there are many more to come.'

'You mustn't tire yourself,' Beth urged, holding back her tears with difficulty.

Her mother smiled contentedly. 'I'll sleep

203

better now that I've seen you,' she murmured. Her eyelids drooped, then she
forced them open.

'You'll remind your dad about those
letters, Beth?' she said so softly that her
daughter had to strain to hear the words.
'He always liked to work to instructions,
and there's one for Will, too. I'd like to have
seen him, but he'll know what to do.'

'I'll see to it, Mother, I promise,' Beth
assured her, her voice breaking.

Janet Stewart saw the look of distress on
her daughter's face.

'You mustn't feel sorry about all this, lass.
I don't. Now, ask your father to come back.'

Beth did as she was bid, and Rob Stewart
crossed to the bedside to hold his wife's
hand, stooping to kiss her forehead.

Beth clenched her hands so hard that the
nails bit into her skin, but she managed not
to break down.

'You've been a good husband,' Janet
murmured, 'and now you must be strong
for the family.' She smiled faintly at her
daughter. 'You're a good girl, Beth. Have I
told you that before?'

With these words, Janet Stewart closed her
eyes for the last time...

The Stewart family sat about the room like
statues, all caught up in their own private
grief. The funeral was over and kindly

neighbours had gone.

Rob Stewart sat at the window, reading Janet's lengthy letter, composed over many months. As he did so, his shoulders seemed to sag.

'Why didn't I see it?' he reproached himself. 'In my eyes, your mother seemed like a rock. She never had an illness in her life – not even a cold.'

Will crossed the room to lay a hand on his father's shoulder. 'You're not alone, Father. We'll all do our best for you. My clearest picture of her is watching her stir that iron porridge pot of hers...'

Suddenly, everyone had their own reminiscences of Janet Stewart, all of them good memories.

'Ay, she was a fine woman,' Fergus McCallum announced with solemnity. He had been one of the first to arrive at the Stewarts' home. He'd brought with him two of his sons, and they'd been joined by Will and Mhairi with little Catherine, leaving the other brothers to cope with his fleet of fishing boats.

Now, Fergus, too, came across the room towards Rob.

'I'll do everything I can to help. You know that?' he said gruffly.

'Ay, thanks, Fergus,' Rob nodded. 'At the moment I can't seem to take it in.'

Only little Catherine remained unaffected

by the tragedy. She slept fitfully in her cradle in the corner. Every now and then, Fergus would rock her gently.

Beth had spoken little since her mother's death. There had been no time to dwell on the past, or indeed upon the immediate future. There were duties to attend to, sandwiches to be made for the crowds of mourners who had flocked up to the Stewarts' house to pay their respects. Mhairi and she had poured endless cups of tea.

Now, thankfully, with one exception, only family remained. She turned wearily towards her sister-in-law. 'I think, if you don't mind, I'll go outside for a breath of air...'

Mhairi nodded compassionately. It seemed obvious that Beth had kept her emotions under control for long enough.

As the girl slipped out through the back door, Mhairi watched another figure detach itself from the mourners and follow.

Beth headed straight for her sanctuary – her father's potting-shed, to be alone. She threw herself on to the old, battered settee, then, head in hands, wept. Tears that had refused to come since her mother died now ran freely down her cheeks...

Again and again, over the past few days, she had asked herself why had she not seen the signs of her mother's illness. How could she have been so blind?

It was all very well for their family doctor

to insist that nothing could have been done for her mother's heart, that it had just worn out. That was cold comfort for someone who prided herself on her nursing skills.

And, of course, what Mother suggested in her letter to Beth seemed impossible.

Lost in her grief, Beth didn't hear the door open or the soft tread of feet on the sandy floor.

Shaun sat down and quietly gathered her into his arms, holding her until her sobs slackened and finally ceased.

'It's your turn now, little one,' he comforted her. 'Cry as much as you must. Your tears have been too long in coming.'

Shaun understood, she told herself thankfully. He knew how much she'd loved her mother, how she'd been holding on to her self-control so that she might at least carry out one of her mother's last wishes – 'There must be no recriminations.'

'I've been watching you in there, dashing round, keeping a stiff upper lip, but you're not in hospital now,' Shaun continued. 'You don't have to put on an act for me. Remember, I know how it feels.'

'I don't know what I'm going to do, Shaun,' she told him, clasping and un-clasping her hands in agitation.

'You'll know, when the time comes,' he assured her.

'But in her letter, Mother says I've not to give up my career, no matter what happens...'

There! It was out at last. With her family responsibilities, how could she do as her mother asked?

'I can't continue working, Shaun, Dad needs me,' she explained.

Shaun tilted his head to one side and thought for a few minutes.

'There's an answer to every problem, Beth, although I can't think what yours is right now. We won't solve them all at once. Take time before you come to any decisions,' he advised.

'You're a kind man, Shaun. To think that I once doubted you...'

'You'd a right to doubt me, Beth,' he agreed. 'You all had – and with cause. Look how your family have accepted this great tragedy ... with courage, but I was the worst sort of coward.'

Beth blinked away the last of her tears. 'What do you mean, Shaun?'

He was looking through the window of the potting-shed with unseeing eyes, as though gazing back into the past.

'There are similarities, Beth. I've been thinking about them all week.' Shaun kept his head averted from her as if afraid to let her see the truth in his eyes. 'When Rosa discovered she was pregnant, I was working high in the Rockies blasting tunnels,' he said. 'There was an emergency on, as usual. I didn't get home for weeks.

'Rosa was always so patient, never a complaint about me being away such a lot, just making sure she was there for me when I came home. Men are thoughtless. I should have seen her fading away before my eyes, but I just put it down to her condition.'

Shaun turned and took hold of Beth's hands.

'She had small hands, too, just like yours, Beth, and she was very beautiful. "My Spanish Lady", I used to call her. Blue-black hair, pink cheeks and the darkest of eyes...' He stopped suddenly, swallowing hard.

'You must have loved her very much, Shaun,' Beth prompted gently.

'I did, but I suppose I should have known it was too good to last. Her mother was a beauty, too, and I'd been told she died at thirty-four,' he remembered. 'Anyway, when I did come to a decision, Rosa was already six months pregnant. I thought I could solve everything by taking her home to my mam. She would look after Rosa all right. Had she not brought up four strapping sons?'

Now that Shaun had started talking about his past, a bitter tirade came tumbling from his lips.

'She had my baby, Beth, and died in doing

so. I don't think I'll ever be able to forgive myself. You see, she was always ready to do what was asked of her, leaving sunny Spain when her own mother died and her father emigrated to find work. She followed me around, too, living in shacks and boarding-houses, then even to Ireland where the dampness crept into her soul,' he finished, his head bent.

'I think you've forgotten one important point,' Beth told him.

Shaun looked up.

'Rosa did those things because she wanted to,' the girl reminded him, 'because she loved you and that was what her life was all about.'

'Maybe so, Beth, but that doesn't excuse me! I should have realised what was happening.'

Beth gave a rueful smile. 'As you said, Shaun, there are similarities, for that's how I feel right now. And I have more reason than most to feel guilty – I was trained to observe illness in others, you were not.' She sighed.

'I spoke to our family doctor afterwards,' she went on. 'He explained that Mother had lived with a weak heart for years. She swore him to secrecy. I should have seen it for myself, though. Perhaps I was closing my eyes, because I didn't want to see,' she finished sadly.

'What a pair we are, Beth,' Shaun shook his head. 'Anyway, some good may come out of all this yet.'

Beth raised her eyebrows questioningly.

'We've learnt we must never take things for granted any more,' he explained. 'At least, I trust we won't make the same mistake again, especially if they affect the people we love. I've been thinking about Julie a lot lately.'

'And?'

'When my contract's complete, I'm going to take her to Spain. Rosa's father went back to Seville. I've been writing to him regularly. When Julie's old enough to travel, we'll visit him.'

'That will be nice,' Beth heard herself say quietly, but her heart was breaking. She remembered her mother's words before she died.

Perhaps that nice young man, Shaun, will be the right one.

Yet, here another hopeful chapter in her life seemed poised to end...

Shaun had proved a tower of strength over the past few days. He'd also been supportive to her father, who seemed a broken man.

No longer did he enthuse about the railway extension in which he'd placed such faith.

Shaun had already told Beth that her father was considering retirement. Fortunately, he had managed to steer him away from that idea. Going back to work was the only way a man like Rob Stewart could cope with sorrow.

'I don't think he should go back to work quite yet,' Beth said. 'Father and I will need time together to work things out. The Company will understand, won't they?'

Beth hadn't admitted that she, too, was considering giving up work.

'Are you all right?' Shaun asked her now.

'Yes,' she told him quietly, 'I'm all right.'

'You're a smart girl, Beth. You'll do the right thing,' he promised her.

Please let him go on thinking so, Beth prayed, for there were still plenty of uncertainties in her own heart.

'I Can't Do Without You'

Mhairi and her father decided to remain in Fort William after the McCallum brothers returned to their father's fleet in Mallaig.

Since the birth of Catherine, there had been several changes in Mallaig. For one thing, Fergus now employed a capable housekeeper to clean his house and cook for his bachelor sons.

This allowed Mhairi to spend more time with Will and their precious baby daughter.

After having lived such a busy life in Mallaig, cooking and cleaning for her father and brothers, Mhairi felt almost guilty with this new-found freedom.

It was Beth's life that now seemed to be collapsing around her.

Shaun Nolan often dropped by when he was in town on railway business, and at first, Mhairi believed the tunnel foreman had come to keep Rob Stewart informed about progress on the extension.

Now she was beginning to realise there might be another motive. Given the slightest opportunity, the Irishman would seek out Beth's company, but Mhairi felt disappointed when she watched Beth's reaction. For some reason the girl appeared to be erecting a barrier.

This was probably due to their recent bereavement, yet Mhairi felt sure Beth had a deep affection for the Irishman.

When her concern made her broach the subject with her sister-in-law, Beth had remained tight-lipped.

Mhairi wished with all her heart that she could help – but how?

Beth was sewing by the light of the lamp on the window-ledge one evening, when she saw Shaun hurrying up the path from the cutting. It was almost a week since his last visit.

Although she had been deliberately keeping her feelings in check, her heart gave a lurch of anticipation.

She glanced at the clock. It was almost nine, a strange time to be calling.

'Father's out,' she explained as Shaun came hurrying in, bringing with him a draught of wintry air.

She felt suddenly nervous at his closeness. 'He's hardly been over the door since the funeral,' she rushed on, 'but it was our Will's birthday today, so they all decided to go down to the hotel for a meal. I'm watching little Catherine until they return.'

She pointed to the cradle in the corner.

Before she could say more, Shaun held up his hand.

'It's you I've really come to see, Beth,' he said. 'I thought you'd want to know.'

'What's happened, Shaun?'

'There's been another accident, at the tunnel head.'

'Serious?' she began anxiously, and he nodded.

'It's been chaotic back there. I've been so busy trying to arrange things, I was unable to come down the line to tell you.

'You see, it was the boss's son who was involved. Young Malcolm was brought to the camp hospital four days ago. We all thought he would die,' Shaun went on.

Beth's hand flew to her mouth in horror. She'd met the contractor's son once. He'd seemed a clever and enthusiastic young man, determined to give his all to the work on the line.

'Malcolm McAlpine?' she repeated. 'Whatever happened, Shaun?'

She busied herself with making tea. Shaun drank thirstily but seemed anxious to tell his story.

'You'll remember McAlpine's brainchild – the water turbine?'

How could she forget? Father had raved about the revolutionary idea. A dam now crossed Loch Dubh and produced the power fed to the workings by a series of pipes. New rock drills were now in use in all the cuttings and tunnels.

'There was an explosion,' Shaun explained. 'The young boss was bombarded with fragments and had to be taken to hospital.'

She'd not heard a thing, caught up with her troubles here in the Fort. Suddenly Beth experienced frustration. Her place should have been at the camp hospital to help in such an emergency.

'How did they cope?' she asked anxiously.

'At first, when the doctor examined the lad, he admitted the position seemed hopeless,' Shaun said in a sombre voice.

'Malcolm wasn't expected to last the night, so we telegraphed his father and the camp doctor made the lad as comfortable as possible.'

'And?' Beth urged Shaun to go on, the nurse in her itching to know what had taken place.

'Well, by morning he was still hanging on, but by now we'd received a telegram from Concrete Bob to say a surgeon from Glasgow was on his way to Lochailort.'

Beth's jaw dropped when Shaun named the surgeon. Everyone in the medical world knew of his brilliant reputation.

As Beth continued to listen, all her old enthusiasm for her job was returning.

How she wished she had been there to assist!

After all, that was why she'd joined the camp hospital in the first place. With renewed poignancy she remembered her mother's letter – *Continue with your nursing, Beth. If you don't, you'll regret it.*

'Did Malcolm survive?' she asked.

Shaun grabbed hold of her hands.

'Amazingly, yes, Beth,' he continued earnestly. 'The surgeon said he must have had a strong will to live, considering all his injuries. Malcolm has to be transferred to Glasgow for more extensive treatment. That's why I'm here, Beth. Malcolm is on his way right now – by train – to Glasgow.'

The girl gasped. 'But that's impossible! How did he get to the train station? The roads are almost non-existent to travel with such a badly-injured patient!'

Shaun Nolan smiled with pride.

'Eight navvies carried him all the way here to the Fort by stretcher. They're on the train right now and will stay with him until he's in the city,' he finished.

'Oh, I wish I'd been there!' Beth exclaimed.

Then she thought about someone else – Alec Buller! He'd left Lochailort because he considered it a backwater. Now, it seemed ironic that he had missed his greatest opportunity to prove his worth as a surgeon – and all because of his anxiety to advance his career.

Sounds from outside heralded the arrival of Fergus McCallum and Rob, their arms linked.

Beth and Shaun's eyes met. 'Changed days!' she remarked. 'I can remember when those two hardly had a civil word for each other.'

'Ah, Shaun,' Rob greeted him. 'I've just heard the news about young Malcolm. The town's agog! That was quite a feat for the lads, eh?'

Fergus strode across to the corner where his granddaughter was sleeping. The sound of his loud voice wakened her.

'Can I lift her for a bitty, lass?' he asked Beth.

'Of course,' she agreed, her heart warmed

by the old man's tender expression.

She watched as Fergus held the child, tickling her chin until the baby chuckled.

'Oh, my wee pet. I'm going to miss you such a lot,' he said with a sigh.

Rob turned round.

'Ach, Fergus,' he consoled, 'it won't be long before you can take a train all the way to the Fort to visit.'

The door opened and Mhairi and Will appeared, their faces aglow.

'Hello, Will, did you enjoy your meal at the hotel?' Beth greeted him.

'It was really nice, and the four of us got a lot of things sorted out,' he replied.

'Has Father told you, Beth?' Mhairi put in.

'Hold on!' Beth interrupted. 'Told me what, Mhairi?'

'Will is going to bring Catherine III down through the canal. There won't be much of a living to start with, but he says it will grow. He's going to fish for scallops from now on. I'll keep house for him and your dad up here.' Mhairi stopped suddenly and clapped a hand over her mouth.

'Listen to me, rushing ahead of myself. It's just a suggestion, Beth, and only if you agree.'

Rob Stewart explained that over the birthday meal Janet Stewart's letters had been discussed at some length.

'It was her last wish, lass, that you should

carry on with your nursing career,' he reminded Beth.

'I know that, Father,' Beth broke in, 'but I didn't think it was feasible. How could I let you come home to an empty house?'

'You won't have to,' Mhairi told her eagerly, 'and what's more, you'll still have your home to return to during leaves.'

All eyes now turned to Fergus McCallum who was dandling his granddaughter on his knee.

He was the only one in the room who seemed less than happy.

'I suppose it'll be quieter for the baby, without all my lads stamping around,' he admitted. 'Besides, when the railway comes through, I'll need a contact here.' He stared down at his granddaughter.

'This is the one I'll really miss,' he admitted frankly. 'Can I come down from Mallaig and visit her, do you think?'

Beth crossed the room and, to Fergus's great embarrassment, kissed him on the cheek.

'As often as you wish,' she told him.

Afterwards, Shaun followed Beth into the garden and down to the potting-shed.

'I told you, didn't I?' he reminded her. 'Things have a way of sorting themselves out. Now you can go back to work with a clear conscience.'

'There's a new moon tonight,' she remarked. 'Shouldn't we be making a wish?'

Beth knew exactly what her wish was going to be.

Shaun said very little, and Beth's heart sank.

'You're thinking about Julie, aren't you?' she asked quietly.

'Perhaps,' he confessed, 'but more, much more, Beth. I'd like to ask you something very important before we make our wishes.'

A silence filled the tiny potting-shed as they faced each other.

'What was it you wanted to ask me, Shaun?' Beth ventured, her pulse quickening.

For once, the confident Irishman appeared unsure of himself, and Beth's heart sank. Something her mother had written in that moving last letter of hers came to Beth's mind – *If a thing's worthwhile, Beth, it's worth fighting for.*

'Oh, Shaun, I'm sorry if I've embarrassed you,' Beth began hesitantly, 'but you see, my feelings for you have become too important to ignore. I should have realised, I suppose, that they could only be one-sided. You made it plain enough that the love such as you had for Rosa comes only once in a lifetime.'

'Beth, please!' Shaun tried to speak.

'No, Shaun, hear me out, then you can tell me what you wanted to say,' the girl insisted, trying to keep her voice steady.

Shaun turned away from the window and, for a moment, Beth could hardly distinguish his face. She felt grateful for the darkness – it helped her to continue.

'Remember when you came to live at our house, Shaun, all those years ago when you were just sixteen? You didn't realise it, but I hero-worshipped you. I suppose it was because you didn't treat me like a child. We had those wonderful trips into the hills together and fishing in Gowdie's burn,' she recalled.

Shaun remained silent, and she faltered for a moment before continuing, 'You must have thought me naïve, with all my questions.'

Perhaps Shaun realised what an effort her confession was costing Beth, for he moved closer, took her hands in his then held them tightly to still their trembling.

'A lot of water has flowed under Gowdie's bridge since then, Beth,' he murmured.

She nodded.

'Yes. We both grew up. I met Alec Buller. Then you came back, Shaun, and my feelings for Alec were put into perspective. Even he noticed my interest in you, questioning my motives for seeing you so often,' she revealed. 'I denied that there was anything between us, of course, only friendship, and to begin with perhaps that was true.

'Recently, though, I've realised that my feelings for you are deeper than that. I thought you felt something, too.' She took a deep breath. 'Shaun, if I was wrong, please tell me. You've been a good friend to me, but I must know how I stand.'

'Have you finished?' he asked.

She nodded.

She was unwilling to catch his eye in case she read rejection there.

'Well, little Beth, now it's my turn,' Shaun began.

With her emotions almost at breaking-point, Beth scarcely dared to breathe.

'When I arrived here in Fort William from Ireland, I admit I was at my lowest ebb. At that point in my life, I was convinced there could never be another woman in my life, not in the special way Rosa had filled mine.'

Inwardly, Beth squirmed with embarrassment. How could I have been so foolish, she reproached herself. I should never have revealed my feelings. How humiliating!

Suddenly, she felt Shaun's hands upon her shoulders and looked up at him.

'But, Beth, since then I've made a discovery. There can be many types of love. Rosa was like a sudden burst of sunshine, flooding my life for a short time, filling my existence with her warmth.

'You, Beth, became dear to me but for another reason,' he said softly. 'You're like a second skin, part of me I can't do without.'

Beth's tension began to ebb away as, almost afraid to believe what she was hearing, she took in Shaun's words.

She put her arms around Shaun's neck, but he was determined to finish what he had to say.

'You've become very precious to me, Beth. I keep telling myself it's too good to be true, that it's impossible to be so lucky twice in a lifetime. I planned to tell you how I felt but, my dearest girl, you delighted me when you beat me to it!' he finished.

'Oh, Shaun, then it is true!'

His arms tightened around her.

As she surrendered to his kisses, Beth thought she'd never known life could be so sweet.

After their declaration of love for each other life took on a new and brighter meaning for Beth and Shaun, as winter gave way to spring then to a glorious summer.

The huge viaduct at Glenfinnan took shape. Thousands of men worked on the greatest feat of engineering the Highlands had ever seen.

On several occasions, Shaun or her father would take Beth along to watch its progress.

It was a spectacular structure. No wonder Rob Stewart had raved about it. Tall white pillars reached up one hundred feet to give the structure a cool elegance. Twenty-one spans curved their way across the Finnan valley, and the concrete used to build them contained rock from excavations elsewhere on the line so that its colour would blend with the terrain.

At the Stewart cottage, life settled into a more leisurely pattern. As time passed, Mhairi became an important figure in the household.

She gave birth to a second daughter, and there seemed only one name to call her – Janet.

Beth thought wistfully how proud her mother would have been of her namesake.

Eighteen months later, a baby boy called Fergus put in an appearance, and Rob Stewart and Will began to talk about building a wing on to their overcrowded house.

Fergus McCallum was counting the months until the extension to Mallaig opened. Then, he assured them, he would become a regular visitor to his grand-children.

When the extension was originally planned, only two main tunnels had been envisaged. Eventually, eleven had to be excavated, which meant that Shaun had less and less free time. Beth, too, was extraordinarily busy, for there were always emergencies on the sites, accidents due to work being carried out at such a pace.

Weekends spent together in the Fort became precious to the young couple, and yet frustrating, because they never seemed to be alone. There never seemed to be time to make plans, and therefore Beth and Shaun, too, began to count the months until the extension would be complete.

Some nights when Shaun was working near the Lochailort area, he would come up to the hospital and he and Beth would go fishing. The tree-fringed loch had become their special place where they could indulge in their dreams.

'You know, Beth,' Shaun said on one occasion, 'when this work is over, I'll more than likely have to leave this beautiful country and travel to the ends of the earth.'

'I know that,' she told him as she rewound her line. 'I've always wanted to see how they look.'

Shaun studied her thoughtfully. 'After Rosa died, I promised myself that I would never ask anyone to share that sort of life with me.'

'Well,' Beth retorted, 'you'll just have to change your mind, Shaun, for I'm coming with you, wherever you go! I've not waited all this time just to be left behind!'

Then came the day when a middle-aged Irish couple arrived in Fort William on the midday train from Glasgow, in ample time for the official opening of the Mallaig extension, now only two days away. Beth and Shaun were on the platform to greet them, then escort them to the Stewart cottage.

A toddler clung to her grandmother's long skirt, peering out occasionally to watch as the young couple made their way towards them.

Julie Nolan was four years old, just a couple of months older than Catherine Stewart. She looked up shyly as Shaun held out both arms.

Beth's heart contracted as the little girl stared apprehensively at her father, who had been absent from most of her life.

It was plain to see whom she resembled. Even at her tender age, Julie had a foreign look about her. She had a mass of dark, wavy hair, held back by a red ribbon. Her luminous black eyes were enormous in her elfin face.

That day, Beth made herself a promise. If it were in her power to do so, she would see that this little girl had all the love – and more – she needed for a happy life.

Beth took to Shaun's parents straightaway. Hard-working farmers, they were completely down to earth. They were obviously devoted to their granddaughter, but under no illusions. Once Shaun was able to take up his responsibilities as a father, they knew that they must part with her.

The first day of April 1901 was one that the people of Mallaig would always remember. Fishermen in their droves were out to wave off the first-ever down train on the extension as it departed for the south.

Two hours later, it passed the first up train from Glasgow bringing passengers for an experience of a lifetime on the new railway.

The Stewarts and the Nolans boarded the train at Fort William, waiting for a fresh engine to be attached.

With little Julie in her arms, Beth held her breath as the locomotive rumbled its way over the Lochy viaduct, then reached Banavie Junction. The train now worked its way around the elbow bend of Loch Linnhe and Loch Eil, then across the Caledonian Canal on its pivoted swing bridge.

The sight of her homeland from a completely new viewpoint, with Ben Nevis towering above, gave Beth a sense of surprise and delight.

Dermot Nolan, an older edition of his son, Shaun, had some doubts, expressed in his rich, Irish voice.

'It seems sinful to disturb such a perfect spot with a smelly steam engine,' he remarked.

'Try telling that to Fergus McCallum!' Beth exclaimed. 'Mhairi's father can't wait for today's opening. He's appointed Will his official agent in Fort William and plans to be the first fisherman to send his fish to market by rail.'

Rob Stewart, for all his long history connected with this line, had been remarkably silent since they boarded the train at Fort William.

Beth, looking across at him, knew that he was thinking about her mother. How often had he promised his dear Janet a window seat on the first train to Mallaig!

There was no doubt that the journey was magnificent. The Nolans admitted it was something they would never forget, even the nerve-racking curve of the Glenfinnan viaduct.

They had passed so many lochs on the way that they had lost count, but when the line met the Atlantic, at Loch Nan Uamh, everyone exclaimed in awe.

Here, the hills swept down to a sparkling sea. Trees were almost tropical in their brilliance where the Gulf Stream brought warmth to the western bays, in complete contrast to the barren wilderness of Rannoch which the train had passed through just three hours before.

Home again, the Stewart household talked non-stop about their enchanting journey.

Dermot Nolan admitted that he, too, had become bewitched, having observed sights from the railway-carriage window that could never be seen from elsewhere.

Meanwhile, the hospital at Lochailort was closing down as the mass of workers left. When Bridget O'Malley expressed concern about her future, Robert McAlpine assured her there would be a job for her when the Company moved on to their next contract.

The building of the West Highland Line extension had made the Scottish engineer's name, and his skill with mass concrete now seemed in high demand.

The Irish girl, who had matured since she came to work at Lochailort, seemed delighted, especially since her brother, Bryan, had also been lucky.

Having married Morag Grey one year before, he'd become an upright citizen, in his sister's opinion. His father-in-law had spoken for him, and Bryan was given a job on the new railway as assistant to the signalman at Banavie – with a possible railway cottage to go with it.

It was Sunday, and Beth's official weekend off. She set out on her own across the hill, carrying a basket of wild blooms and some grasses. Sometimes, Shaun would accompany Beth on this pilgrimage but, although she would never say so, she preferred to come on her own.

She walked slowly to her mother's grave, now graced by a white, marble stone. *Janet*

Stewart, it read simply, *Died 1898.*

Where had the years gone, Beth mused. Sometimes when Mhairi and Will were out, and the children asleep, Beth would wander through the house, remembering past times. She felt closest to her mother whenever she was in the kitchen, where Janet Stewart's hand-printed recipes were still pinned to the wall beside the range.

Now, Beth knelt on the grass beside the grave and began to speak quietly.

'The Nolans were so nice, Mother. I think they liked me well enough.' She crossed to a well and filled her vase with water then returned. 'Do you remember what I told you about Shaun, last month? Well, he got a reply to his letter yesterday. His old firm have offered him a job. Mr McAlpine put in a good word.

'Anyway, he's going to be blowing holes in mountains again – in the Pyrenees, would you believe?'

Beth had the strange feeling that, if she were able, Janet Stewart would have been questioning her right now.

'I don't know, Mother, honestly I don't. He's never really pinned himself down to a date for the wedding.' Beth looked down at her left hand. The ring Shaun had given her two Christmases ago had a little ruby in the centre surrounded by tiny sapphires.

'All right,' she agreed at last. 'I'll put it to

him the moment I go home. I know what you're thinking.'

Beth found that she always went home in a more positive frame of mind after her imaginary conversations. She rose from her knees and brushed away the grass from her skirts, feeling she'd made the right decision.

Mhairi's father was coming by train for tea. He would be staying for the week, and it meant rearranging all the rooms again. Mhairi didn't really mind. She looked forward to his visits nowadays. She knew he did, too.

Never had she known a man to change so much. With the birth of his grandchildren, Fergus McCallum had grown almost affable. Catherine was his favourite, there was no denying that, but Janet had found her own way into Papa's heart with her constant demands to be told tales of the sea, and whenever he was allowed to hold young Fergus in his arms, Mhairi would watch the gleam of anticipation in her father's eyes.

'I wonder what he'll be when he grows up?' he would say.

Not another fisherman, Mhairi would pray quietly. She'd got used to her inland ways. Loch fishing was fairly safe and appeared to satisfy Will's need for a deck beneath his feet. With all his family responsibilities now, he had decided to diversify, and was talking of starting up his own depot here, in the Fort, to act for all the fishing villages that used the Highland Line.

The extension on the railway was now complete, but Mhairi Stewart's was not. Masonry was heaped at the side of their house and one wall had still to be finished.

One Sunday the talk was all about the mass of workers leaving the area. It was sad really, Beth said. There was practically nothing to do up at the hospital these days, just the odd cut or scratch. All those skilled men being lost to the area!

'I could do with a few of them here, to finish that wall out there,' Mhairi said with a rueful smile.

Shaun looked up. 'Could you, now! Well, I know some men who could throw that lot up in a wink with me to supervise.'

Beth gave her fiancé a warning look, and he had the grace to flush.

'I would only be a couple more weeks, lass. What would that mean after the time we've already waited?'

Everyone around the table stopped talking and looked up expectantly.

Shaun grinned. 'We've set the big day, you see. It's the first of June,' he announced.

There was a great cheer, and Rob Stewart clapped his hands.

'About time, too,' he declared. 'I was beginning to believe I would never walk Beth down that aisle.'

Mhairi offered to make Beth's wedding dress. She'd made her own, she confided in Beth, and still had the headdress. Now, that could be something borrowed!

There would be no shortage of flowergirls, either. Catherine and Janet talked about nothing else, and of course there was the dark-eyed little girl from across the Irish Sea.

'We'll need those extra rooms when our guests arrive,' Shaun reasoned, as Beth stared out of the window to see all his friends hard at work.

She had hoped these last few weeks could have been free of disruption, so that she could prepare peacefully for her wedding day, but it was not to be.

The men had set-to with a will, but there had been extra work for the womenfolk, with all the cleaning and keeping dust out of the house.

As Mhairi went out with plates of potatoes and stew for the workers' lunch, Beth turned to Shaun. 'Is everything settled, then?' she asked.

Her fiancé patted his pocket.

'Tickets, passports, the lot!' he assured her.

Beth gave a long sigh. She'd been waiting for this for so long, yet now she felt almost nervous.

It was such a big step, leaving the place she had known all her life, leaving her mountains and lochs, the family she loved.

'You're not having cold feet, I hope?' Shaun said gently, attuned as he now was to her every emotion.

Her shoulders went back in a gesture he had come to know well. 'Don't you believe it, Shaun Nolan! It's going to be a grand adventure!'

Their honeymoon would be a short one on Skye, then it was off to the blue skies of Spain and to the Pyrenees.

Little Julie Nolan was going with Shaun and Beth to meet her Spanish grandfather, before Shaun started his new job.

For once, the house was empty, the young ones out with Will and Mhairi for a sail on Catherine III.

Shaun and Beth sat close together on the window-seat and made their final plans.

'Oh, Beth, my darling girl,' he murmured. 'I never thought it would all come true. It's like a fairytale.'

He looked at her with eyes filled with wonder.

Beth looked like a princess today, with her burnished hair newly washed and brought into order for the big day tomorrow. Her skin glowed with health and happiness, and there was a sparkle in her eyes that held nothing but joy and love for him. They made a handsome couple.

Shaun had not been allowed to see the finished wedding gown which Mhairi and Beth had been making.

This hung on the back of Beth's bedroom door, and if he'd seen it before the big day there would have been a risk of bad luck. But how could anything connected with Beth Stewart bring him other than joy? He blessed the day he met her, and all that had happened since.

Suddenly, he was jerked from his day-dreams.

'Do you realise we're wasting precious time, lass?' he demanded.

'What do you mean, Shaun? This is the first chance I've had to sit still all day...'

'That's what I mean. I've been watching you on the move all day. But now we're alone. The workmen have finished and your family are out.'

Beth chuckled, but as she lifted her willing lips to his, her busy mind was remembering something important.

If I get a chance tonight, when everyone is asleep, she decided, I must slip out and tell Mother about all our plans. I'm sure she'll approve.

This Large Print Book for the partially sighted, who cannot read normal print, is published under the auspices of

THE ULVERSCROFT FOUNDATION